A Candlelight
Ecstasy Romance ®

**"JAIME, YOU'RE DRIVING ME CRAZY,"
HE GASPED AGAINST HER PARTED LIPS.**

She took great gulps of air, inhaling the warm, musky scent of his skin. She wanted Mac badly. But slowly, reluctantly, she dropped her arms to her side and stepped back from his reach.

"I'm not some little blonde who'd willingly fall into bed at your slightest touch. Oh, I realize that you see me as a challenge, but I'm afraid this is one challenge you'll have to lose."

Mac's smile stung her in every raw nerve of her body. "You're a lovely lady and a very sexy one. I'd like you to know I don't usually do this sort of thing with my employees, but I felt you were special. I still do. I'm also a patient man. I can wait until the time is right. . . ."

CANDLELIGHT ECSTASY ROMANCES ®

FOR BETTER
OR WORSE

Linda Wisdom

A CANDLELIGHT ECSTASY ROMANCE ®

Published by
Dell Publishing Co., Inc.
1 Dag Hammarskjold Plaza
New York, New York 10017

Dell ® TM 681510, Dell Publishing Co., Inc.

Candlelight Ecstasy Romance®, 1,203,540, is a registered
trademark of Dell Publishing Co., Inc.,
New York, New York.

ISBN: 0-440-12558-8

Printed in the United States of America
First printing—June 1984

To Our Readers:

We have been delighted with your enthusiastic response to Candlelight Ecstasy Romances®, and we thank you for the interest you have shown in this exciting series.

In the upcoming months, we will continue to present the distinctive sensuous love stories you have come to expect only from Ecstasy. We look forward to bringing you many more books from your favorite authors and also the very finest work from new authors of contemporary romantic fiction.

As always, we are striving to present the unique, absorbing love stories that you enjoy most—books that are more than ordinary romance.

Your suggestions and comments are always welcome. Please write to us at the address below.

Sincerely,

The Editors
Candlelight Romances
1 Dag Hammarskjold Plaza
New York, N.Y. 10017

CHAPTER ONE

"Don't you think you just might be a little overqualified for this position, Ms. Clarke?" the man's deep, raspy voice asked as he looked over her résumé.

The woman seated across from him exuded a cool confidence that equaled his own. A pair of smoky gray eyes, fringed by dark lashes, looked unfalteringly at her interrogator.

"If I had felt that I might be, Mr. MacMasters, I wouldn't be here wasting either your time or mine." Her soft voice held the faint hint of a Southern drawl. Jaime Clarke sat back in her chair, appearing the picture of ease, even though her stomach was churning madly. "You advertised for an accountant with five-plus years experience; I have six. You asked for someone who has been in on a conversion to computer; I not only supervised a conversion, I checked out the various firms to see what computer would be our best bet. You wanted someone with supervisory experience; I had six clerks under me. And I also have the added advantage of having worked in a construction firm." She presented him with a cool smile, still the confident woman.

John MacMasters, Mac to his friends, leaned back in his chair rubbing his bearded jaw in an absent gesture. He couldn't help but admire this woman's supreme self-confidence. It almost seemed that she was in charge of the interview, not he.

Damn, she was beautiful! he thought, making sure nothing in his manner gave his thoughts away.

When Jaime had met Mac thirty minutes earlier, she hadn't guessed she was meeting the heart of MacMasters Construction. Mac's faded old jeans, and worn T-shirt, as well as his unruly coal-black hair and beard, spoke of a worker, not a company owner.

What had unnerved her the most were his eyes, a deep cobalt blue with a hint of purple around the iris and the thickest eyelashes she had ever seen on a man. She had an idea that without the beard he would be an extremely handsome man, not that he wasn't good-looking now. Now he just appeared very masculine, sexy, and somehow dangerous. She schooled her features not to betray any emotion, knowing he was watching her with a razor sharpness that wouldn't miss the tiniest movement she made.

Jaime resisted the urge to shift in her chair and smooth the front of her skirt. She couldn't let him know how important it was that she get this job. Her creditors were already getting upset that she could afford to pay only a fraction of what she owed. If she didn't get a job soon, she'd be in deep financial trouble in a matter of weeks. While Mac studied her résumé, she took the time to examine him a little more carefully. His tall body fit easily in the large leather chair. The strands of silver in the dark hair and beard, along with the lines fanning out from his eyes and mouth, told her he had to be in his mid to late thirties, probably the latter. The strong, callused fingers that now held a pen were a reminder that this man had worked his way up in the industry with hard labor and not a fat bankroll.

"I gather there's no problem in your working late, then." His voice was a husky purr that danced along a woman's nerves. "Correct me if I'm wrong, but doesn't an accountant always put in a great deal of overtime at least once a month?" Mac continued.

He wants to know if I'm married or have a boyfriend hanging around, Jaime thought with a hint of amusement. "There's no such thing as a forty-hour week for an accountant," she stated, meeting his direct stare.

Since that tactic didn't work, there were always others. "I should think that the cut in salary would bother you," Mac said, his eyes roaming over Jaime's spice-colored raw silk suit as if he could discern the designer label sewn into the jacket.

Her eyes narrowed slightly. This man was baiting her and enjoying it, but she wasn't about to give him the satisfaction of letting him know he was succeeding. He undoubtedly knew there were more accountants in the job market than there were jobs. Actually, the fact that she had drawn an extremely high salary at her last position had only made it more difficult for her to find another job. Most prospective employers thought that she'd accept their job only to leave when a better-paying one came along. That was not for her, thank you. She wanted a job and if she got one, she'd be willing to stay there for the next hundred years.

"If it bothered me as much as you think it does, I wouldn't be sitting here right now," Jaime said crisply. This wasn't an interview, this was a game, and right now the score was tied. She had already guessed John MacMasters to be the type of man who was used to making all the rules himself. So far the interview had been proof positive.

"We don't have a large accounting department here," he informed her, interrupting her thoughts. "I have three clerks, and a CPA comes in once a month to balance the books, although with an accountant here, I doubt he'd have to come in more than a few times a year. I need someone to be in complete charge at all times. I don't want some lightweight who will come running to me for permission every time a check needs to be issued. I prefer spending my time on the job site, not behind this desk."

That accounted for the dark tan and casual clothes, Jaime thought. She had already guessed him to be one of those rough-and-tumble men she didn't care to have anything to do with. She had learned a long time ago that the brains of such men were

11

usually lodged in the muscles they enjoyed showing off to anyone who cared to look.

"You're the first person I've interviewed for this job and there's several more for me to see, so I won't be making my decision for a week or so. I'll be in touch, Ms. Clarke," Mac said, ending the interview. The smile on his face was unsettling.

Jaime slowly rose to her feet. She held out her hand and flashed him a cool, impersonal smile, then said, "Thank you for your time, Mr. MacMasters."

His own smile seemed to mock her cool formality as he stood up and took her hand. "My pleasure, Ms. Clarke," he said a bit too intensely.

As she left the office, Jaime had had to exert every ounce of self-control she possessed to suppress an unaccountable desire to run from the room. She had a strong feeling that Mac's eyes were on her every inch of the way and and an even stronger feeling that he was enjoying the view. Outwardly, however, she looked unhurried as she descended the redwood stairway to the first floor and the reception area of the small building that housed MacMasters Construction.

Sue, Mac's secretary, looked up and smiled at Jaime, who returned the smile automatically, hardly aware of the other woman's presence. She was too busy concentrating on keeping herself together. When she had applied for the position as accountant, she hadn't expected the owner to be so disturbingly virile and sexy. Mac's rough masculinity and rugged attractiveness had kept her completely off balance. Even the beard did nothing to detract from his looks, she thought in amazement.

"What do you think?" Hearing Mac's question, Sue looked up from the letter she had been typing to find her boss standing next to her desk. "Think she'd add some class to the joint?" he asked with a smile.

She brushed a gray-streaked curl away from her face before replying in a dry voice, "Probably too much." She narrowed her eyes at the speculative look on Mac's face. "Hey, boss, watch it,

I know that hungry look of yours. She's way out of your league."
She continued with blunt familiarity. "That young lady belongs
in a plush office in a big high-rise, not here with us peasants."
In Sue's opinion, her age—fifty-three—and length of service
with Mac—gave her the right to speak so bluntly.

A faint smile played about Mac's lips. "What if I told you that
before this year is out, I intend to marry that lady?"

Sue's expression was filled with pity, as if she thought Mac had
been spending too much time out in the sun. "Eleven months or
eleven years, it won't make any difference. She's caviar and we're
pretzels. I just bet every piece of clothing she had on carried a
designer label. You can't afford her, Mac. Besides, I don't know
where you got the idea she'd have anything to do with you." A
thought occurred to her. "Wait a minute, did you already offer
her the job?"

His eyes danced with amusement. "Not yet, but when I do,
she'll accept. I can feel it. You have no faith in me, Susan, my
love," he chided in an affectionate voice, stretching his arms over
his head with a lazy animal grace. "I'm going out to the site,
where I am more appreciated. I signed those letters and left them
on my desk. I'll see you in the morning." He walked out with
backward wave of the hand.

"Hopefully you'll have gotten more sense by then," she called
after him.

Meanwhile, Jaime had steered her gunmetal-gray Porsche
onto the Pacific Coast Highway, heading for her home in South
Laguna Beach. Even though it was mid-January, the day was
sunny and warm, made for being out enjoying the good weather
instead of inside an office interviewing for a job. Unless, of
course, you needed the money to keep gas in the car and the rent
paid.

The cool, rational part of her was warning her that Mac
spelled trouble, while her reckless self urged her to jump right
in. Sure, it's a small company and the salary wouldn't be as much

13

as she'd been getting before, but she felt that John MacMasters might give her the chance she hadn't been given before.

Jaime downshifted and turned onto the steep, winding road that led to her small house. The rent was outrageous for the tiny one-bedroom home, but it had a spectacular view of the sea and Jaime had more privacy there than she would have had in an apartment. She parked her car in the carport and walked wearily to the door, contemplating a hot bath and a glass of wine to help her relax. Jaime hated interviews because she knew she had to sell herself. This one, however, was even worse than usual: The man looked as if he were definitely buying!

Once inside, her first stop was the bedroom, where she slipped out of her suit and into a dull gold caftan. She brushed her dark-red hair, which feathered to just past the nape, free of tangles.

Jaime couldn't resist smiling as she remembered her meeting with Mac. At five foot six plus her high heels, she rarely had to look up too far at a man. With him, she most definitely had to tilt her head back to see his face. He had to be well over six feet.

Padding barefoot out to the small living room, she switched on a classical station on the stereo. She poured herself a glass of wine and walked into the bathroom to start her bath water. Her head snapped up when she heard a knock on her front door and a man's voice calling out.

"Jaime, hurry up! My arms are full and I'm almost dropping our dinner!"

Laughing at the sound of the familiar voice, she hurriedly turned off the taps and ran to the front door. When she opened it, a sandy-haired man handed her one of the bags he had been holding.

"Fish and chips," he announced. "You're not going to let a man bearing food stand outside, are you?"

"What are you doing here?" she asked, still laughing. As she took the bag from him, she suddenly looked very different from the cool and composed woman who had been sitting in John

14

MacMasters's office an hour before. "How did you know I'd forget about dinner? Neil, you're a life saver."

"Just part of my Boy Scout training. Besides, you've always been forgetful about food when you've had something important on your mind." He walked into the kitchen. In no time he had transferred the fish pieces and french fries to two plates. "You have any more wine?" he asked, eyeing the glass Jaime held in her hand.

"It's Gewurztraminer."

Neil grimaced. "Too spicy for my taste. I guess I'll have to rough it and have a Coke instead."

Jaime shook her head. "Hot or iced tea or coffee. I'm afraid the cupboard is pretty bare."

"I take it your interview didn't go very well."

"It depends on who you're talking to," she said candidly. "John MacMasters isn't your run-of-the-mill company president."

"Meaning?" Neil set the plates on the breakfast bar, pushing one in Jaime's direction as she settled herself on one of the round leather stools.

"Meaning no three-piece suit, who knows the last time he saw a barber. He more or less resembles a grizzly bear," she said, sprinkling salt over her french fries and picking one up to munch on. "You forgot the catsup. It's in the cabinet next to the stove."

"Sorry." Neil's apology was dry. He opened the door and pulled out a tall bottle. Holding on to the bottle, he continued to watch her closely. "He got to you, didn't he? One interview and this guy got to you."

"I'm so glad I'm not one of your patients who pay good money to listen to you blabber on like this. Especially when you only talk nonsense," Jaime told him in a bored drawl, refusing to admit that he might be the tiniest bit correct. "I wouldn't be at all surprised if your students fall asleep during your lectures."

"Ouch." He winced. "Obviously the rumors have left the campus." As a well-known psychologist and part-time lecturer

15

at the University of California at Irvine, Neil Hamilton was in great demand. He rested his elbows on the counter. "You could quit all this worrying about finding a job so quickly if you'd reconsider my offer and move in with me," he suggested.

"I don't think Karla would appreciate an unwanted third," Jaime retorted dryly.

Neil heaved a mock sigh. "She's in Orlando for six weeks." As a troubleshooter for an international computer firm, Karla Fields traveled a great deal.

Jaime's laughter was rich and full. "Oh, now I see why you're here! If you're so lonely, why aren't you out having the time of your life?"

"Because she's the only one I'd like to be out with," he said with a sigh. "Also, if she found out, she'd kill me." He leaned over and ran the tip of his finger down her forehead and over the line of her pert nose. "When is your turn coming? I just know that somewhere out in this cold, cruel world is a man who's going to take you in tow and destroy all your misconceptions about the male sex. I only hope that I'm there to see it. You are one very stubborn woman. Madam, I could help you so much if I could just get you on my couch!" He leered playfully at her.

Jaime was more than used to Neil's teasing. After all, she had grown up with it. They had known each other since Jaime was six and had always been as close—if not closer—than any brother and sister. They still shared that closeness. When one had a problem the other was always there to help.

When he left after dinner, Neil thought about offering Jaime a loan, but he knew her stubborn pride only too well. If she was without a job for too much longer, though, he would insist that she take something.

When Jaime was alone again, she took her bath and then curled up on her periwinkle-blue couch with her checkbook and calculator. It didn't take her long to figure out how much longer she could live on the money she had left, including the rapidly diminishing sum in her savings account. If only she hadn't splurged on that cruise last fall! If it gets any worse, she might have to sell the Porsche. She heaved a deep sigh and rested her head against the back of the couch.

Jaime soon found her thoughts running back to her meeting with John MacMasters. A tiny smile tugged at the corners of her mouth. The man was definitely dangerous. At the same time, he tempted her. What would it be like to work for man like that— someone who didn't mind getting his hands dirty? She'd bet the pink slip on her car that he was also someone who never lacked for feminine company.

"A big grizzly bear," she murmured. "And no one in their right mind would want to tangle with a grizzly."

The following week was quiet for Jaime. Unsure of what to do next, she applied to several employment agencies, but all they told her was that positions at her level were at a premium. Though there were several possibilities in the newspaper's classified advertisements, nothing turned out to be worthwhile. She might have had better luck if she wanted to drive into Los Angeles every day, but that would be a last resort. With every passing day, she was growing more and more discouraged. A part of her had expected to hear from Mac before now, but by now she despaired of his calling.

By the following Monday, Jaime was beginning to fear that she'd have to call her mother and ask for a loan. But that meant she would have to explain why she had left Trenton Construction. Of course Neil would lend her money, but his expenses were pretty high since he had recently bought a house. She had been surprised that Mac hadn't asked her reasons for leaving Trenton, unless he had already known. If so, why hadn't he mentioned it?

After spending the morning cleaning and waxing the kitchen and bathroom floors, she was ready to scream with frustration. When the telephone rang, she grabbed the receiver with eager hands. At this point she'd even be happy to go out on an interview.

"Ms. Clarke?" The deep, rumbling voice was one not easily forgotten.

Jaime drew a deep breath. Why did this man unnerve her so? "Good morning, Mr. MacMasters." Her voice came out even and formal.

"I gather you haven't found a job yet." It was more a statement than a question.

Jaime winced at his blunt choice of words. He certainly didn't believe in sparing a person's feelings. "I don't like to jump at the first thing that comes along. I do admit that I'm surprised to hear from you," she prodded gently.

"Do you think you can be here at seven in the morning?" The question sounded like a command.

She gripped the receiver tightly as if afraid she might have heard wrong. Would this be her chance? She desperately hoped so.

"Of course there are a few details we'd need to iron out first," Jaime said calmly, deliberately keeping her voice matter-of-fact.

"Such as?" Mac asked, his tone suspicious.

"Such as an employment contract."

"*What!*" Jaime held the receiver away from her ear, wincing at the deep voice blasting her eardrums.

"An employment contract," she repeated patiently. "Such as, if I'm to have full control of the department, I want it in writing. Also, if anyone tries to interfere where they aren't supposed to, the contract is void and I leave without any repercussions."

"You've got all this figured out, haven't you?" There was no denying the admiration in his voice. "I guess this is your idea of job security, no matter what happens."

Her haughty tone carried over the phone lines. "It's done in all the best companies, and it's the only way that I'll work for you." Jaime inhaled a sharp breath, silently cursing her too-quick tongue, certain that Mr. MacMasters would say he was no longer interested.

"Be here at seven sharp, Clarke." Mac turned brusque. "One

18

thing I don't tolerate from my employees is lateness." Without another word, he hung up.

Jaime slowly replaced the receiver. She couldn't remember accepting the job, but it seemed, like it or not, she was John MacMasters's new accounting manager.

She picked the phone up again and hurriedly punched out a number.

"Neil? Pick out your favorite restaurant. It's my treat," she said, smiling broadly.

"Who died and left you a fortune?" he demanded. "Or, should I say, who hired you?"

"MacMasters Construction."

There was silence on the other end. "Are you sure that's what you want?" he asked finally.

"I know I said I wasn't sure I'd take it if it was offered, but after this long I can't be too choosy."

"Hm, this should prove interesting," Neil mused. He remembered the faint flush in Jaime's cheeks when she first mentioned the firm—and its president. He was sure there was more to her reaction than met the eye.

"Behave yourself or I'll tell Karla on you," she scolded. "I'll pick you up at seven."

Humming to herself, Jaime hung up and gathered up her cleaning supplies. As far as she was concerned, she now had more important things to do.

When Jaime entered the A-frame two-story building the next morning, Sue was already at her desk. The older woman looked up from her typing and smiled brightly.

"Hi," she greeted her. "I hear you decided to join the zoo."

"In a manner of speaking." Jaime's voice was dry as she recalled her conversation with Mac.

Sue grinned, interpreting her thoughts. "Yes, Mac can be a bit much at times, can't he? I'm Sue Ellis. I'm not only the secretary here but also the receptionist, switchboard operator, den mother,

19

and general gofer." This was one woman who scorned the idea of middle age.

"All of that must keep you pretty busy," she commented, smiling at the woman's easygoing banter.

"Only if you're working a twenty-five-hour day." Sue picked up the phone and punched out a number. "She's here, boss, and if you're not down here in two minutes, I'll relate every horror story about you I know and then begin making up a few."

"Are there that many stories around?" Jaime asked after the secretary had hung up.

"Volumes and still adding on, but no one ever believes me." She looked Jaime up and down. "This time I sure can't give Mac any argument."

"About what?" Jaime asked curiously.

"That you'd give the place some class."

Jaime spun around at the sound of the raspy voice. Today the jeans Mac was wearing were even scruffier than the ones he'd worn during her interview and his T-shirt was a faded blue instead of yellow. His dark blue, almost purple eyes moved leisurely over Jaime's café-au-lait silk shirtwaist dress and dark-brown suede blazer. Suddenly she felt awkward and overdressed. Funny, from the way Mac's eyes were twinkling, she'd swear he read her mind.

"We'll end up as a five-star establishment yet, Sue," he said as he gazed at Jaime. Then he turned to his secretary. "Don't think you can scare this lady off with some of your horror fiction either. I have an idea she doesn't frighten easily. Am I right, Clarke?" He spun around abruptly to face Jaime.

Only of you, she thought involuntarily. You could frighten me. Aloud she said, "Never show fear to your boss is my motto."

Mac's lips twitched. He was clearly enjoying this. "Come on back and I'll introduce you around and show you to your office."

"Say, King Kong, while you're back there if you find a razor, will you please use it? I'm tired of that pelt you call a face," Sue called after them.

Mac chuckled as he led Jaime down the hallway. "I came back from a two-week hunting trip with my beard and Sue hasn't let a day go by without telling me how much she hates it. She's even told me she hopes I get fleas!"

If he didn't have the beard, Jaime thought, he would probably have to shave twice a day. Now, why would that matter to her? Why should she even worry about what the face beneath the beard looked like? In the confines of the narrow hallway, she could detect the hint of a spicy soap and a scent that was definitely all male.

"I like your perfume, Clarke," he murmured. Had he read her thoughts again?

"You had mentioned something about wanting to convert your accounting system to computer." She was determined to keep this conversation on a businesslike footing.

"That's right, although I sometimes wonder about the so-called infallibility of the computer. I'm a paper-and-pencil man myself." He followed her lead. "One thing I was impressed with was your previous experience in converting. I figured I'd just leave it up to you to check out the various systems and come to me when you've found the right one."

"Of course." Though she'd worn her highest heels, she still had to tilt her head back to look up at him. Why did he have to be so damn tall!

Mac chuckled softly but said nothing as he opened the door and stepped back to let Jaime enter first. "You've got great legs, Clarke, among other assets," he murmured as she passed him.

Jaime spun around, her eyes flashing angrily. She slowly and deliberately let her gaze wander down Mac's broad-muscled chest, to his surprisingly lean waist, then down to his hips and thighs. "You're not so bad yourself, MacMasters," she returned flippantly. "In a primitive sort of way."

Even her cool appraisal didn't faze him. "Easy, Clarke. If *you* were the one to ask nicely, I just might shave off my beard."

21

"No, as long as it doesn't drag along the floor, it's fine with me." She smiled sweetly. "Could we continue the tour now?"

Mac shook his head, still laughing softly. "You can even put a man down in a nice way." He swept out one arm. "Along here."

Jaime was beginning to wonder if Mac also owned a glass company, judging by the large number of windows. The mountains in the distance were clearly visible. The view was a picture more breathtaking than any painting.

"My office crew," he announced. "Gina, Carrie, and Marie. Ladies, Jaime Clarke, the ogre I brought in to crack the whip since I'm too soft-hearted to even yell at you. Gina handles the payroll; Marie, the payables; and Carrie, the receivables. They also pitch in for everything else. Since I can't add two and two, even with a calculator, I rely on them to keep things under control. Your office is back here."

Jaime could find no fault with the comfortable working area. Her desk was oak with a rust-color padded chair. A calculator sat next to the telephone. She glanced around, inspecting a painting of a desert scene on one wall and several plants that hung in front of the window. The room was exactly the way she would have decorated it.

"If there's anything you need, let Sue know and she'll get it for you," Mac told her as he watched her walk slowly around the office.

"The first thing I'll need to do is go over the books and familiarize myself with your accounts," she informed him crisply. "I also want to assure your staff that I'm not here to make any big changes, unless I can improve the system. If all goes well, I can have a report for you by the end of the week."

Mac nodded. "By the way, I'm having Sue type up your employment contract now. She'll bring it in when she's finished and you can look it over. I'll be out of the office for the rest of the day, but as I said, if you need anything, just let her know."

Alone, Jaime wandered freely around her new office, trailing her hand over the polished wood of her desk. Even Trenton, for all its money, didn't have anything this nice for their accountants. She turned when a tentative knock at the door sounded and Gina opened it a crack.

"How about some coffee?"

"Sounds fine." Jaime smiled warmly, appreciating her friendly suggestion.

"Good." Gina pushed the door open wider and walked in carrying two steaming mugs. "I wasn't sure if you took cream or sugar," she said as she held a mug out. Then she settled herself in the chair opposite Jaime's desk.

"Just black, thanks." Jaime accepted the mug and sank down into her chair.

"Mac said you'd want to go over the books but warned us not to overdo it your first day. I think he's afraid we might scare you off." Gina's fingers fluffed her short cap of dark-brown hair. Dressed in jeans and a pale-green shirt, she resembled a pixie, especially when a wry grin curved her lips.

"How long have you worked for Mr. MacMasters?" Jaime took an experimental sip of the hot coffee and found it strong but good.

"Six years. Marie's been here for five and Carrie, two," she replied. "Before that, Sue handled all the bookkeeping until it grew so much that Mac needed additional people." The dark-haired woman watched Jaime closely. "Mac said you'll be converting our system over to computer."

She nodded. "I understand you're using pegboard now. I don't think you'll really have too much trouble converting."

"You may as well know now that I'm the plain-spoken one of the group. We're all wondering which one of us will be replaced by the computer," Gina stated bluntly.

"Thank goodness there isn't any beating around the bush here," Jaime said lightly. "Haven't you heard that it usually takes more people where a computer is involved? The paperwork never ends."

"You'll hear some loud sighs of relief then." Gina grinned. "We've been sweating this out for the past week."

Jaime felt confused. "For the past week?" she repeated in a faint voice, although there was no change of expression on her face. "Oh, you mean since Mr. MacMasters began interviewing for an accountant?"

"Ever since he interviewed you and told us he had found the person he was looking for. He spent all last week putting this office together." Her eyes twinkled impishly. "You must have really impressed him."

Jaime thought back to Mac's statement about interviewing several candidates. If he had started work on this office right away, he hadn't even waited to think it over. Then why had he waited so long before he contacted her?

"Well, I'm sure the others out there are chewing their fingernails waiting for the outcome. Shall we go out and put them out of their misery?" She reverted to her crisp and businesslike manner. Marie and Carrie both turned out to be very friendly but it was easy for Jaime to see that Gina was the leader among the three clerks, and the most knowledgeable about the business. Jaime kept busy all morning scanning ledgers. She decided to work straight through the afternoon to get through as much as possible.

Sue dropped off the employment contract and explained that Mac would be returning that day after all and would see Jaime at three thirty. Before she left, she asked if Jaime would like to go out to lunch.

"I'd like that," Jaime responded, genuinely pleased to have been asked. She hadn't been prepared for the friendly office. The female clerks in the accounting department at Trenton had resented a woman accountant and the men only saw her as a schemer who would do anything to get ahead. This time, however, Jaime was determined to prove to everyone that she had the brains to run a department in a businesslike, efficient way.

At lunchtime, Sue eyed Jaime's Porsche with envy. "I knew

I should have stayed in school and gotten my degree," she commented wryly, sliding into the bucket seat.

"Why didn't you?" Jaime asked, sliding behind the steering wheel and switching on the engine.

"I met Ray, my husband, and married him six weeks later. Raising four boys may have driven me out of my mind at times but it also ensured that I didn't get stuck in any kind of rut. When Mac offered me this job, I grabbed it quick. Ray's one of Mac's foremen, although it wasn't all that long ago that Mac worked under him for another firm," Sue explained.

Jaime decided to wait until they reached the nearby Mexican restaurant before prodding Sue further about their boss.

"If your husband worked with Mr. MacMasters before he began the company, he must have known him a long time." She threw her casual comment out as she ate her tostada.

"Um, about nineteen years," Sue replied, dipping a tortilla chip in salsa. "Mac was nothing more than a green kid who was ready to fight the world when Ray met him. That husband of mine has always had a soft heart, and he decided to take Mac in hand. This was one time when it paid off. When Mac decided to strike out on his own, he asked Ray to come work for him. Times were rough in the beginning, but we've never regretted it. One thing I have to say about Mac is that he always takes care of his friends. He may have taken a big chance to go out on his own, but he made sure that no one else would be hurt by it."

"You make John MacMasters sound as if he could qualify for the hero of the year award."

Jaime's dry sarcasm was lost on Sue. "He's the best man you can find." She was sincere in her praise.

For the remainder of the lunch hour, Jaime continued to casually pump Sue but didn't learn anything more. She refused to admit that her curiosity wasn't about Mac as an employer but as a man. Though she was a little irked by the knowing looks Sue threw her way, she pushed them out of her mind. It was obvious

25

Sue thought highly of Mac and that in her eyes he couldn't do any wrong.

Promptly at three thirty, Jaime knocked on the door to Mac's office and opened it at his gruff order to enter.

She crossed the office and laid the signed contract on his desk.

"You're extremely generous, Mr. MacMasters," she informed him. "Some people would read this and think that I'm a very demanding woman."

Mac's dark eyes moved lazily over her slender figure. "I imagine you could be," he murmured suggestively.

Jaime couldn't stop the flush that spread over her cheeks, but she refused to allow her reactions to color her voice. She already knew that she would be better off ignoring Mac's innuendos. Who knows? Perhaps it was some type of test to prove she could work in this office.

"I'll have that report for you by the end of the week," she stated, keeping her voice neutral. "Is there anything else?"

"Not just yet, Clarke." Mac leaned back in his chair looking totally at ease.

Jaime clenched her teeth, turned, and walked out, fully aware that Mac was watching her leave.

"Oh, Clarke, you've got a nice a—"—he paused deliberately —"walk."

Jaime halted for a moment then she continued. It took all of her self-control not to slam the door behind her. This could prove to be more than she reckoned on.

CHAPTER TWO

Jaime arrived home that evening wanting nothing more than to kick off her shoes, find some dinner, and spend a quiet evening by herself.

After a shrimp salad and a glass of white wine, Jaime turned on the stereo and curled up on the couch. She tucked her bare feet under the warm folds of her sapphire-blue velour robe, looking very much the picture of relaxation.

Jaime's brow creased in a thoughtful frown as she remembered her day spent with her new boss. It would be so much easier for her if Mac weren't so rugged-looking and attractive. The beard was what added the ruffian look to him, and those eyes! She drew a sharp breath. She was positive many women had fallen under the spell of the liquid purple in those dark-blue, heavy-lashed eyes. What a crime to waste them on a man!

"I must be crazy to even think of such a thing," she muttered, leaning forward and reaching for her glass. Sitting back, she idly twirled a lock of stray hair. A smile touched her well-shaped lips. If nothing else, working for John MacMasters certainly wouldn't be dull!

Jaime's days were busy as she familiarized herself with the accounting system and jotted down suggestions for improvements. She was determined to be more than prepared when she presented her report to Mac.

"You don't need to work all this hard, you know," a deep voice murmured as she sat poring over paperwork.

Jaime looked up from her notes and flashed her visitor a cool, impersonal smile. "I do if you want me to do my job properly, Mr. MacMasters."

Mac raised his eyebrows as he lowered himself into the chair across from her. "Still so formal," he commented. "What would it take for you to call me by name?"

"I thought that's what I was doing." Didn't he own anything besides decrepit jeans and T-shirts, not to mention cowboy boots that looked older than he did?

"I've been out on the site all morning." Again he seemed to read her mind with an accuracy that was unnerving.

"You must like to keep an eye on everything," Jaime replied, leaning back, her arms resting lightly on the chair arms.

"I don't believe in letting my men think I sit behind a desk all day and count money," Mac replied brusquely. Then, with a swift change of subject, he stated, "I thought we'd have lunch." It wasn't a request, more a royal command. One Jaime felt tempted to jump to her feet and salute.

She knew better than to question Mac about this sudden invitation. She simply glanced at the small digital clock on her desk and said, "I'd like to be back by one."

"Don't worry, I'd never keep a stylish lady like you out late." Jaime glanced at him with surprise. Mac gestured toward her designer jeans and dull-gold silk blouse. "They may be jeans but they're sure not like mine," he said. There was no rancor in his tone. He stood up. "Think you can get away now? After all, you are going with the boss."

Jaime nodded and opened a drawer to get out her purse. She'd grab her coat on the way out.

Mac had brought along a well-worn sheepskin-lined suede jacket. He slipped it on as he led her outside to a battered dark-gray pickup truck.

"I guess it's a far cry from your Porsche," he said, nodding toward her car as he assisted her inside the cab.

"I'm sure yours is much more appropriate for your work," she replied, looking around at the worn yet comfortable interior.

Mac climbed in next to her and half turned in her direction. "Don't patronize me, Clarke." His voice was rough silk on her ears.

It took every ounce of Jaime's self-control to silently battle his unwavering gaze. "As you're the one who signs my paycheck, I wouldn't dream of doing so," she replied evenly.

He waited another long moment before he turned away and started up the engine. Jaime wondered where Mac was taking her during the silent drive down the Coast highway. They were in an area she wasn't all that familiar with, but it wasn't long before she discovered their destination. He parked the truck in front of a small coffee shop and got out to walk around and help her out of the cab.

They walked inside and sat down at a table in the back.

Mac grinned at Jaime. "They've got the best chili dogs in town here," he told her. "Guaranteed to burn the roof off your mouth."

She glanced around the small interior whose dingy walls were decorated with movie posters from the 1930s. Probably they were used to cover the worst spots where the paint had peeled off the walls or where there were holes in the plaster, she decided. As she turned back, she thought she noticed an assessing look in Mac's eyes.

Then all the pieces fell into place. He was testing her! Mac had expected her to kick up a fuss over his bringing her to this hole in a wall. Well, she'd show him who'd win this round!

Flashing him a cheerful smile, she commented, "I guess there won't be any problem in having onions on mine, will there?"

A spark of humor glittered in his eyes, although it didn't echo in his voice. "None at all." This lovely woman was turning out to be much more than he expected. Mac silently admitted that he wouldn't have been surprised if Jaime had taken one look at the place and insisted that she wouldn't set one foot inside. Some of the women he had taken out certainly wouldn't be as accommodating. Oh, yes, this woman was different. Now all he had to do was convince her of that fact.

Mac proved to be entertaining company. He informed Jaime that he had eaten many a lunch and dinner there when he had been a construction worker.

Biting into her chili dog, she found out Mac had been more than accurate about his description of the food. The many spices ferociously attacked her tastebuds. Fighting the tears in her eyes, she thirstily gulped her Coke.

"How's your mouth?" Mac grinned, taking a huge bite out of his second chili dog and picking up a large handful of french fries.

"You should be charged with arson," she croaked, when the heat in her mouth lowered to a simmer. They sat in their corner, unaware that they were being watched by the other occupants. They made a good-looking, although incongruous, couple—with Mac dressed in his dust-covered work clothes and Jaime resembling a high-fashion ad. There was also a spark between them that no outsider could miss.

Gazing up at his broad-shouldered frame, Jaime tried to visualize him in a three-piece suit and conservative tie, but try as she might, the vision couldn't materialize satisfactorily.

"It won't work," Mac said with a smile as he leaned back in his chair until it was propped on its two rear legs.

"What won't work?"

"Picturing me in a suit." Again he had perceived her thoughts! She hadn't thought her face was that open. "Shirts and ties on me don't mix. If there was a way I could run my business on the site and do without an office, I would. I'm not a desk jockey. I'm a man who needs to be outdoors, and the only way I can safely do that is to have a capable crew in my office. You might as well know the only reason I'm trusting you so much with the financial

30

end is because of your impressive record and equally impressive references. You're highly thought of in your field."

"For a woman," Jaimie murmured wryly. Silently she wondered who at Trenton would have given her a good recommendation. Certainly not Ron. The last thing he would have done was give her a good reference.

Mac's eyes centered on the curve of her breasts visible beneath the silk blouse. "I freely admit that's an obvious fact, but you're still an excellent accountant or I wouldn't have hired you." The solemn expression on his face backed up his statement.

"Is that why you keep the beard? Because it seems to belong more in the wilderness than in a business office?" Jaime didn't want him to realize how much his mind reading disconcerted her.

Mac idly stroked the dark beard, drawing Jaime's attention to his lean, dark fingers. "A beard didn't hurt Lincoln any," he mused. "It's also good during the winter to keep the face warm."

"True, you never can tell when we might have a blizzard," she said dryly.

"No, for something like that I prefer a willing woman." That remark effectively ended the conversation.

Jaime watched with silent awe as Mac ate four chili dogs along with a large order of french fries and several cups of coffee.

"Don't forget I'll burn all of this off by midafternoon," he said, skillfully interpreting the expression on her face.

Having already noticed his flat stomach and lean waist, Jaime didn't doubt his words.

"If you want to be back by one, we had better get going," Mac said, glancing down at his watch.

Outside, he assisted Jaime into the truck then walked around to the driver's side. She leaned back in the seat feeling deliciously full.

"After all that spicy chili and onions I ate, I won't dare go near anyone for fear of destroying them." She chuckled.

A thumb and forefinger captured her chin and turned her face

31

to one side. Jaime stared, mesmerized by the purple lights dancing in his eyes.

"Don't worry, I can handle it. I'm not just anyone," Mac whispered as mouth lowered and his tongue probed her lips.

Jaime's pulse halted then sped up under his delicate yet sensual touch. This was no ordinary kiss, she realized. It wasn't meant to tease or to explore. It was a kiss that promised much more, that challenged her and demanded a deep response. The hairs of his beard didn't scratch her face as she had expected, but rather lent an erotic caress of their own. She hadn't expected a man's beard to be so soft and sensual, and so strangely comforting.

Jaime wasn't exactly sure when Mac had unfastened the front of her blouse and slid his hand inside to move under the lacy material of her bra. The hard, callused thumb circled her nipple in a lazy caress that sent a warm ache to the center of her body. Intense heat seemed to radiate from Mac's body, burning into hers.

Jaime's fingertips stroked over his shoulders. She could feel the play of muscles beneath her sensitive exploration. Her palm glided downward, unerringly finding the spot over his heart measuring the rapid beats. When he finally pulled away, she couldn't miss the ragged sound of his breathing, loud in the silence surrounding them.

"Personally I think the chili tastes better on you than on the hot dog." His husky voice came out raspier than usual. His hand slowly left her swollen and aching breast and pulled the edges of her blouse together before he carefully buttoned it. The palm of his hand rested momentarily over her left breast and he smiled as he felt the rapid heart rate that matched his own. His thumb then moved up to rub over her moist lower lip. The tip of Jaime's tongue moistly caressed the roughened skin and her lips drew it into the depths of her mouth, grazing it with her teeth.

Her mind was whirling from her intense response to him. She had dated more than her share of men, none of whom were novices in the art of seducing a woman, but not one had created the volatile response that Mac had; and it frightened her.

"That was a mistake," she said quietly after taking a moment to compose her voice.

Mac slowly shook his head as he ran his thumb over the edge of her teeth, then lifted it to his mouth for a brief heart-stopping moment. "Not as far as I was concerned," he murmured. Then he turned back to the steering wheel and switched on the engine.

Jaime was glad for the respite in order to pull herself together. The last man in the world she would have thought could raise her blood pressure was John MacMasters, yet in a matter of seconds he had transported her into a mindless world and left her yearning for his slightest touch. This man was far more dangerous than she had thought. She decided she must never repeat the fatal error of allowing him to get too close to her.

They hardly spoke during the ride back to the office. Each was completely lost in thought.

Damn, why had he tried that so soon! Mac wondered as he drove. She was beautiful, sexy, one of the most desirable women he had ever met; but now he'd probably ruined any chance he ever had with her. What was it about this woman that made him lose control so easily? He couldn't even have lunch with her without wondering what her kiss tasted like. His hands twitched slightly as he recalled the soft skin of her breasts and how easily her nipples had responded to his touch. What did they taste like? Silk and honey, like her mouth? He silently cursed himself for getting into this. If he was smart, he'd stay out of the office for the rest of the day. Mac was glad to see that they had almost reached the office; he wasn't sure how much more of this tense silence he could take.

"Thank you for lunch," Jaime said politely when Mac helped her out of the truck.

"You get an A for etiquette," he murmured close to her ear, as they walked inside the building. "But you flunked humanities."

Jaime was saved from replying by Sue, who looked confused as she said, "Oh, Jaime, am I relieved to see you!" She waved her telephone receiver in the air. "There's a man on the phone who claims he needs to talk to you. Something about you're having to return to the Home?" She clearly thought the caller was a prankster.

Amused, Jaime shook her head, already knowing who was on the line. "I'll take it." She picked up the receiver and pressed the button emitting a flashing light. "Really, Neil, couldn't you have been a little more inventive?" she chided the caller.

"You mean you knew it was me?" He pretended to be hurt. "She said you were at lunch and I thought that would guarantee you calling me back right away."

"I just got back and I've really got a lot of work to do," she pointed out, refusing to look at Mac, who was standing much too close to her.

"All right, I get the hint. I just thought you might want to get out as much as I do, and since Karla's still out of town and you're the only woman she trusts me with, I thought you might like to see *A Midsummer's Night Dream* or whatever they're calling the new version. I was able to get tickets for tonight's performance."

"Tonight? I don't know how you got so lucky, but I'm not going to argue. What time will you pick me up?" After hearing his reply, Jaime made some rapid calculations in her head. She stood with her back to Mac and missed the dark scowl on his face as he unashamedly listened to the conversation. "I'll see you later then."

"No offense, but your friend sounds a little crazy," Sue said, taking the phone from Jaime and replacing it in the cradle.

"Neil just likes to sound that way. Actually, he's a clinical psychologist and teaches at UCI," Jaime replied. "He's been trying to get tickets for *A Midsummer's Night Dream* and finally got lucky. This is a modern-day version and was a hit on Broadway."

34

"Sounds very intellectual," Mac observed with unconcealed scorn. "Both the play and your boyfriend."

Jaime's gaze was a little derisive. She decided not to bother correcting his assumption about Neil. "I admit it isn't Saturday morning cartoons, which I'm sure must be more your speed. Neil is a highly intelligent man and well thought of in his field."

"Probably boring as hell," he gibed.

Ignoring him, Jaime walked down the hallway to her office.

"It sounds as if you lead Norman around like a puppy on a leash," Mac taunted her. "Tell me, does he 'roll over' and 'heel' too?"

Jaime spun around. "His name is Dr. *Neil* Hamilton, he has an IQ of one sixty-five and is the author of several well-known psychology textbooks," she informed him coldly. She saw no reason to tell Mac that she and Neil weren't lovers. Why should she care what he wanted to think?

Mac's eyes bored through her. "Meaning he's just the type of man for a sophisticated woman like you," he said slowly. "Not some kind of ordinary workman like me, right?" Without waiting for a reply, he turned and strode down the hall, his back stiff and erect.

For a moment Jaime was tempted to call out and apologize, but why should she? Who said she had hinted Mac was inferior? Why did he act so hurt?

"Jaime." Sue's quiet voice came from behind. "I know you weren't belittling Mac, but it may take him a little time to realize it. He's worked hard to get where he is and he's working twice as hard to stay there. He's a proud man and like any proud man, he doesn't want a woman to see him in a bad light. Just pretend it never happened and everything will be fine."

"He's not proud, he's stubborn," she murmured.

Sue smiled. She had an idea things weren't going to be the same around there from then on.

Jaime walked back to her office. She had already decided it was too hard to try to figure Mac out. At the moment, she wasn't too sure about anything except that if she didn't get back to work soon, she wouldn't be able to get out of there on time.

When she arrived home that evening, she hurriedly showered and changed into a burnt-orange silk dress, then brushed her hair and freshened her makeup.

As usual, Neil was punctual, handsome in a dark-blue suit.

"How's the new controller of MacMasters Construction doing?" he greeted her, stepping inside at her invitation.

"Controller? I'm the accounting manager, if that. There really isn't enough there to warrant a controller." Jaime picked up her suede evening bag and got her wool coat out of the closet. "MacMasters hired me much too soon, from what I can tell."

"Maybe he liked your legs," Neil teased, helping her on with her coat. "Or was it your work background that piqued his interest?"

Jaime thought back to Mac's remark about her walk, although it wasn't her legs that had drawn his comment. What rankled was that he had been aware that she knew exactly what he had been thinking.

"He isn't the type of man to bother with a woman's intellect," she snapped, not caring to discuss her boss any further. "We don't want to be late, do we?"

Taking her hint, Neil led her outside to his Jaguar coupe.

Despite all her best attempts, Jaime didn't enjoy her evening out. Her thoughts continually returned to Mac's burning kiss and the heat of his hands as he held her. Even the memory was enough to send tingles along her spine. Her hand twitched in her lap and she fought the urge to reach up and touch her lips the way Mac had earlier. She shifted restlessly in her seat, crossing and recrossing her legs.

When the play ended, she clapped automatically with the rest of the audience. She didn't remember one word spoken.

"I made dinner reservations at your favorite restaurant," Neil told her as they left the theater. "All the sushi you can eat."

36

Jaime smiled at his thoughtfulness. "You hate Japanese food," she pointed out in a gentle voice.

"True," he agreed readily. "It's amazing how you women walk all over me. I just thought it might be nice for you to have a special evening out. You don't seem to have too many of those anymore."

"It's purely by choice," she informed him dryly.

Neil's eyes on her were a little shrewd, but wisely he said nothing.

Jaime soon discovered she couldn't enjoy her dinner as she usually did and silently cursed Mac for intruding on her life.

Neil kept up a running conversation during their meal, relating several humorous stories about his students. He continued his chatter during the long drive back to Laguna Beach and Jaime's house.

"Would you like to come in for a brandy or cup of coffee?" Neil affectionately mocked Jaime's silence when he slowed the car in front of her house. "Yes, I would, thank you."

"Don't let it be said that you're not subtle, Neil. No wonder Karla does as much traveling as she does. It's the only way she can preserve her sanity," she said wryly as they walked up to her front door. "All a person can handle is *extremely* short doses of you!"

"Her way is to ignore me when I start getting this way. I've found this manner works best with my students." He followed her inside and settled himself on the couch.

Jaime slipped off her coat and walked over to the liquor cabinet. She poured brandy into two glasses and carried them back to the couch.

"Tell me about your new boss," Neil said, warming the glass between his palms. "Is he the interfering type or is he going to sit back and let you run the department your way?"

"There's nothing special about him." She shrugged and dropped gracefully into a nearby chair. "The typical 'do it yourself macho man' who's raised himself up from a construction

37

worker to the owner of a large and still growing firm. He drives a broken-down pickup truck; his clothes look like they come from an army surplus store, and he probably doesn't have a necktie to his name," she commented. "He's the type of man who snaps off bottle caps with his teeth or tears phone books in half just to show off his muscles." All the time she spoke, Jaime had an unsettling sensation in the pit of her stomach, as if she didn't really believe all the things she was saying.

Neil leaned back and laughed loudly. "You're overdoing it, love. If you're not too careful, I'll think that you're attracted to the man."

"Attracted, ha!" Jaime dismissed his words. "John MacMasters is the last man I'd be attracted to. His type of women probably wear skin-tight satin pants and sequined tube tops and have those breathy voices and an oversized bosom."

"Please!" Neil held up a restraining hand. "I see enough of those on campus. My heart can't stand the strain! I still think you feel an attraction for him, so why not give in to your baser instincts? Smooth out the rough edges and who knows, you might even talk him into wearing a tie," he teased.

She glared at him as she sipped her brandy. What would Neil say if she told him that the rough edges were very much a part of Mac's charms?

"I'm not into affairs," she drawled.

"I believe you've said that all too many times. There must be something drastically wrong with your libido because you certainly don't look like the typical cold fish," he informed her.

"Don't psychoanalyze me, Neil," Jaime warned.

"Can't. I didn't bring my notebook and clock." He grinned. "What a shame, too, because this all sounds very interesting."

"MacMasters is nothing more to me than my boss," she insisted, hoping that she sounded convincing on the outside, because she certainly didn't feel it on the inside.

"Hm, I think I'll have to come down and take you to lunch," he mused. "I'm curious to see this guy."

"If you do, I'll be sure to pick somewhere very expensive," she threatened sweetly. "And Karla wouldn't be too happy to come home and find that budget she and I made up all shot to pieces just because you went a little crazy while she was gone."

"Tell me the truth, Jaime, why did you accept the job?" Neil asked her. "Especially when the guy bothers you so much."

"I couldn't turn down the money," she said bluntly, preferring to ignore his latter remark.

He shook his head in disbelief. "I guess I should go before you decide to tell me to get out." He stood up, walked over to Jaime, and dropped a light kiss on her lips. "My offer to be your roommate still stands," he told her. "Don't let your new boss get to you. Show him some of that hard-headed common sense you're capable of. If that doesn't work, wear shorter skirts."

"Good night, Neil." Her smile softened her abrupt words.

After Neil left, Jaime carried the glasses into the kitchen and then went to bed.

An hour later, she was still wide awake. She had already decided to stay out of Mac's way as much as possible. His kisses were definitely enjoyable. In fact, Jaime was a little worried that she enjoyed them too much. But an affair with her employer, especially a man like John MacMasters, just wasn't her style. She determined to keep their relationship strictly businesslike.

"Definitely no more lunches with the boss," she muttered, turning over and punching her pillow.

CHAPTER THREE

A few days later Jaime called her mother to arrange a lunch date for that day, and at exactly noon, Sue buzzed her to tell her Eileen had arrived. Jaime had to smile at the note of confusion apparent in the secretary's voice. Few mothers and daughters were as dissimilar as Jaime and Eileen.

"Hello, Mother," Jaime greeted the petite brown-haired woman warmly.

"Hello, darling." Eileen smiled fondly at her daughter, who towered over her by several inches.

"Going to lunch, Ms. Clarke?" a rough male voice asked. Jaime hadn't seen very much of Mac in the past few days and had decided that he must be spending all his time at the site. Forcing herself to smile, she turned in his direction. "Yes, I am, Mr. MacMasters. I'd like you to meet my mother."

"I'm pleased to meet you, Mrs. Clarke." Mac flashed her a smile and extended his hand. "Now I see where your daughter inherited her beauty." His eyes twinkled wickedly, plainly enjoying Jaime's discomfort.

"Oh, no, Mr. MacMasters, Jaime is very much her father's daughter," Eileen trilled.

"I won't keep you ladies any longer. Enjoy your lunch. It was nice meeting you." After squeezing Eileen's hand, Mac walked away, his tall, muscular body arresting in the sunlight as he strode across the parking lot to his truck.

"Such a charming young man." Eileen shot Jaime a sly glance as they walked to Jaime's car. "Quite good-looking too."

"I don't know how you could tell, what with that beard of his," Jaime commented in a dry voice, unlocking the door to the Porsche.

"That only makes him look all the more masculine," Eileen said as she seated herself in the low-slung bucket seat. "I think you might even call him sexy."

What an understatement! Jaime thought, but she merely wrinkled her nose and switched on the engine. "A little too earthy for me." She gunned the engine and pulled out into the busy midday traffic.

"I have an idea he would be the kind of man you could count on when things are bad." Eileen's voice grew pensive, remembering her husband's death just the year before.

"Would you like to try that new English tea room?" Jaime spoke up hastily, not wanting her mother to dwell on her sorrow too long. Though she could only guess how much Eileen missed her husband of so many years, she knew that her mother had to keep on living. "Let's not worry about diets today. Let's just stuff ourselves the way we used to after those afternoon orgies of shopping."

"I'm glad to see you enjoy your job," Eileen said as they sat relaxing over their meal. "Although I don't see why you have to dress so casually there." She gazed with a mother's critical eye at Jaime's jeans, shirt, and blazer.

Jaime smiled at her mother's comment about her "casual" clothes; if only she knew how expensive they were. "We all dress casually," she replied.

"It certainly doesn't make you look very ladylike."

Jaime eyed her narrowly. "Now you sound like Neil."

"Neil is a very bright boy," Eileen said complacently.

Jaime suppressed a smile at the idea of thirty-three-year-old Neil called a boy. At the same time, she recalled that Eileen had referred to Mac as a man. An interesting distinction. Then she glanced down at her watch. "I didn't realize it was getting so late. I guess we had better get back. I have a lot of work to do."

"I'm so glad we could get together," Eileen said sincerely when Jaime returned them to the office parking lot. "I don't get to see you very much since you started your new job. I'm glad to see you're so happy in your work."

Poor Mother, Jaime thought. Suddenly she saw the older woman in an entirely new light. She's so lonely and hates to admit it. "Perhaps we should do this every week," she suggested brightly. The way the older woman's eyes lit up was answer enough. "I better get back to work. I'll call you early next week and we can plan another calorie-laden lunch!"

Jaime spent the afternoon figuring cost breakdowns for the materials needed for the Royalton project; Mac needed them as soon as possible.

Leaning back in her chair, she tapped her pencil eraser against her teeth, thinking of Royalton Properties, Inc.

Frederick Royalton was well known for having the uncanny knack of buying up property in an area that would later become very popular. His landholdings in Orange County, outside of San Diego, and in the mountain regions of Lake Arrowhead and Mammoth were proof of that sixth sense. Right now he was preparing to build a large townhouse complex in Dana Point. It was a contract any builder would give his right hand to obtain. Mac had been spending a great deal of time poring over the blueprints and making notes for his own reference.

Jaime sighed and rolled her head from one side to the other to relax the tired muscles in her neck. After double-checking her figures, she used the photocopier in the other room. Everyone had already left for the day, so she decided to finish up and leave her work on Mac's desk. That way he could go over it first thing in the morning.

She wasn't surprised to see a light on in his office when she went upstairs. Lights were usually left on for the office cleaners who came in each night. What she didn't expect was to find her boss hunched over the drafting table. He looked up at the sound of an intruder, then smiled as he pulled off a pair of aviator-style eyeglasses and tossed them on the table.

"Well, well, what a surprise," he greeted her. "Don't look now, but your mouth is open." He noticed her staring at his face. "Someone would think you hadn't seen a man wearing glasses before," he softly taunted.

Jaime obediently closed her mouth, although she still couldn't stop staring. It wasn't the glasses that caused the surprise, but the sight of a new Mac. The beard had disappeared, uncovering angular cheekbones and a rugged chin. She couldn't help but notice that the clean-shaven face revealed a pair of bone-melting dimples!

"I-I didn't know you wore glasses," she said stupidly.

He replied cryptically, "I do a lot of reading. Is there anything else wrong?"

"I guess I just didn't think you'd still be here." Her voice faltered as she strained to recover her composure. John Mac-Masters may have been attractive in a rough-hewn way with a beard, but without it he was devastating!

"I decided it was a good time to get caught up on some of this paperwork. That wasn't what shocked you though, was it? Actually, I think it was the sight of my naked cheeks," he said softly. "Kinda gets to you, doesn't it?" His grin was boyishly wicked.

"Not really," Jaime replied in a cool voice, slowly regaining her composure. She crossed the office and laid the sheets of paper on top of the drafting table. "I thought I'd bring up the first set of cost breakdowns for the Royalton job. That way you can go over them first thing."

Mac glanced up at the wall clock and noticed it was nearly eight o'clock. "Working late, aren't you?"

"Don't worry, I won't put in for overtime," she said dryly.

He frowned and shook his head. "I just don't like the idea of you being here alone so late at night."

43

"You're here."

"That's not the point." He grunted. "Come on, I'll take you to dinner."

Jaime tensed, remembering his devastating kiss after lunch. She had an unsettling feeling that dinner with this man might prove too much for her to handle and was certain he would expect more than coffee and liqueurs afterward! "Thanks, but I have other plans," she lied.

Mac's eyes hardened. "With Nigel?"

She blinked, surprised by the vehemence in his voice. "Neil," she corrected him, wondering why Mac never got the name right.

"Close." He shrugged dismissively and turned back to his work, picked up his glasses and slipped them on. "Good night, then."

Figuring silence was her best option, Jaime left the office and went downstairs. Just before she got into her car, she gazed up at Mac's office window and could see the light shining out over the street. Funny, she hadn't thought of him as a loner before. She had figured him to be a man who needed a woman around him constantly to support his ego, if not his libido. Dismissing her thoughts with a shrug, she slid into the driver's seat and was soon on her way home. All she wanted at that moment was a hot bath and bed.

"There's a rep coming this morning to show me a computer system and I want the three of you to sit in on the presentation," Jaime told the clerks the next morning. "You're going to be using the system also, so you may as well have your say in choosing it."

"Is Mac going to sit in on it too?" Marie spoke up.

"No, I'll give him a report after we've heard all the sales talks." He had been affecting her thoughts in a very upsetting way lately and she wasn't sure how to handle it just yet. Luckily he hadn't wanted to be at these presentations, only to be notified when she had made her decision.

As it was, Jaime wasn't very impressed with the sales talk and dispensed with the representative with intimidating formality. Her office staff had to leave the room so the salesman wouldn't overhear their laughter.

"I apologize for that," Jaime told them after she escorted the man out. "If I had known he was so ill prepared, I wouldn't have bothered setting this up. With reps like him, I don't know how they can stay in business. In fact, to make it up, how about Mexican food for lunch? My treat."

"No one in their right mind would turn down lunch with the boss when she's picking up the tab," Gina said, still giggling. "Did you see how red that guy's face got when you shot down every one of his sales points? I thought he'd explode!"

"Anyone who comes in not knowing his product deserves much more than I gave him," Jaime said grimly, then smiled. "Come on, after a boring talk like that, we deserve a long lunch."

That afternoon Jaime left her office to get a cup of coffee. Noticing a young woman hovering near Sue's empty desk, she walked out to the reception area.

"May I help you?" Jaime asked politely.

The young woman spun around, her bright blue eyes full of impatience. "It's about time," she snapped, lifting her hand to replace a blond curl cut in a deceptively casual style. Mistaking Jaime for the receptionist, she contined coldly, "I'm here for Mr. MacMasters."

Naturally, Jaime thought. Just the type Mac would fall for. Under twenty-five, just barely five feet tall, blond hair and baby-blue eyes. What was it about blondes that had men falling at their feet? "Do you have an appointment?" She spoke in an equally cool voice, drawing herself up to her full height.

The blonde heaved a sigh and tapped her high-heeled foot. "*I* don't need an appointment. Just tell your boss that Miss

Randolph is here. He won't appreciate my being kept waiting, I can tell you that."

Jaime could feel her temper rising. At the same time, she knew she couldn't wish someone like this on Sue. "Just a moment, then." She mentally brushed the young woman aside the way someone would get rid of a annoying fly.

She walked upstairs to Mac's office. "A Miss Randolph is here to see you," she announced.

A slight frown of annoyance crossed Mac's features. "Bambi? What's she doing here?"

Jaime fought down her urge to burst out laughing, although mirth was evident in her voice as she said, "Bambi? You've got to be kidding. Where did you find a child with a name like that? Tell me, do they check her ID when you go out?" she couldn't resist asking.

He flashed her a chilling glance. "I don't take her out anywhere, she's from—" He stopped abruptly. "Look, just tell her I'm tied up and I'll call her later." It was more an order than a request.

"I think we should get something straight here," Jaime's mild voice belied the gathering storm clouds. "I am not your secretary and I certainly don't believe in lying to that poor little girl waiting for you. If you want to get rid of your girl friend, you're going to have to do it yourself." She turned and walked out, shutting his door with a little more force than necessary. She walked downstairs and calmly informed Bambi to go on up, that Mr. MacMasters was expecting her. She then returned to her office.

Ignoring the work in front of her, Jaime collapsed in her chair. She rested her head in her hands and closed her eyes, fighting the headache that was becoming more unbearable by the second. She couldn't remember having these headaches before, at least not before John MacMasters came into her life.

"Bambi," she muttered. "Doesn't take her out, my foot! Then I wonder where he takes her in? Perhaps I should have asked him

46

about her little woodland friends. With a name like that, it shouldn't be difficult to imagine what her line of work is."

"Sorry to disappoint you, but I've never had to pay for my pleasures." Mac's drawl interrupted her thoughts, showing he had overheard her derisive remark.

"At least I knock before I enter someone's office," she said tautly.

He watched her with narrowed eyes. "I think I should talk to Neville—"

"Neil!"

"Whatever. No matter what his name is, you've got a nasty disposition," he told her in a cold voice. "And he needs to do something about it."

Jaime's eyes glinted with anger. Her temper had only been simmering before and if she had been left alone, it would have dissipated. Now it was reaching the boiling point. "I'll make a deal with you, MacMasters," she stated in a cold, no-nonsense voice. "You stay out of my private affairs and I'll be sure to continue to stay out of yours." She sat back in her chair, waiting for him to pounce on her slip of using the word "affair."

"You got it, Clarke," he growled. "And just for the record, Bambi is a college student who wants a job as a secretary. She's been pestering me for an interview for the past three months and I'd been able to put her off until she showed up here today and you very kindly pushed her through my door. Due to you, it will probably take me a good six months to pound it through her head that she needs to learn to type before she can work as a secretary!" He slammed the door loudly as he exited.

Jaime's lips curled. "I bet she knows how to walk out onto a runway."

Jaime was curious to ask Sue if she had ever heard of Bambi, but didn't know if she would want to hear a negative reply. Yet why would Mac have lied to her? Even with all his male arrogance, she doubted that deception was part of his makeup.

For the next few days, Mac and Jaime made a point of staying out of each other's way.

Early one evening, Jaime was working late in her office and wondering why she bothered to push herself so hard. She bent her head to massage the bridge of her nose with her thumb and forefinger and jumped when she felt a pair of hands gently grip her shoulders, rhythmically rubbing the tension from the muscles.

"Didn't I warn you about working here alone at night?" Mac's rough-velvet voice sounded close to her ear.

"I didn't notice the time," she replied, closing her eyes and delighting in his sensuous touch.

"So I've found out." He chuckled softly, his hands still kneading her shoulders. The tightness had evaporated from her muscles only to be replaced by new, more disturbing feelings. Ones she tried not to think about.

"Don't tell me you're not going out with Norman tonight? On a Friday night at that." Mac's voice was heavily laced with amusement.

"His name is Neil and he is lecturing tonight, if it is any of your business, which it isn't."

His hands withdrew abruptly. "Even though I appreciate your efforts to correct your previous mistake, Clarke, it *is* getting late," he drawled.

Jaime turned her head, then wished she hadn't as her eyes encountered the front of Mac's denim shirt. It was unbuttoned to the middle of his chest, exposing a thick mat of black crisp hair frosted with silver.

"Where's *your* hot date for this evening?" she challenged, needing to say something to push back the strange lump in her throat. "I can't see the great John MacMasters dateless on a Friday night."

"My lady's mother unexpectedly came to town for a long visit," he replied smoothly.

48

"Oh, what a shame." Jaime smiled archly. "Don't tell me, let me guess what kind of women you like. Under five foot four, blond hair, big blue eyes, at least twenty-one, and the IQ of a flea. Their names run the gambit of Tammy, Misty, maybe even a Bambi or DeeDee. What fascinating conversations you would have!"

Mac's eyes hardened into two midnight pools. "Actually, Louise is a legal assistant, divorced and trying to raise two kids. She has dark-brown hair and brown eyes and she's thirty-four. Let me tell you something, Jaime. You may have the look of some proper little puritan at times, but your tongue can tear a man to shreds." His voice softened seductively. "I'm sure I could think of much better uses for it." His eyes lingered on the entrancing shape of her mouth.

Jaime could feel the hot color wash over her face. Without thinking, she jumped to her feet and found herself staring directly at Mac's suntanned throat. Why did I decide to take off my shoes? she wondered in a panic. Without them she felt small and helpless compared to him. Her senses began working overtime, aware of the heat of his body. A musky odor of cologne and clean male skin.

"Think of whatever uses you want for it, but don't expect me to play along. I'm not like Louise or anyone else you're used to." Her voice was unsteady, almost quivering, and Jaime wanted desperately to run from his commanding presence.

"No, I'll have to agree with you there," Mac said, laughing at her discomfort. His eyes, however, remained on the V neckline of her rust-colored blouse, which revealed the discreet hollow between her breasts.

Jaime managed to move away from Mac, although her legs felt a little shaky.

"I really can't see any reason to continue this ridiculous conversation," she said carelessly, heading for the coat tree to grab her coat and step into her shoes.

"We could always continue it over dinner," Mac suggested, an intense expression on his face.

She shook her head, refusing to look at him.

"You're making a mistake in not getting to know your boss better, Jaime," he said flatly.

She whipped around. "Oh yes, the old ploy of 'if you want to get ahead, you be nice to the boss,' right? Of course here it means go to bed with the boss," she said coldly. "How pathetically predictable."

Mac's eyes were merciless. "I don't make love to prudes, Jaime." His voice cracked overhead like a whip. "Personally, I think your shrink boyfriend should be analyzing you instead of making love to you. It would be much easier." With that, he spun around and left the office, slamming the door behind him.

Jaime could only stare at the closed door, stunned by the unexpected savagery in Mac's voice. She had seen him lose his temper before, but he had still maintained control. Tonight she watched him almost lose that control. While he hadn't frightened her, she still knew she was better off to remain wary around him. She hurriedly gathered her things together, determined to get out of the building without running into him again.

"Damn!" Jaime muttered, resisting the urge to place a well-deserved kick against the front of her clothes washer. It had been making funny noises for the past few weeks and finally refused to work at all that morning. "Why do these things always happen on the weekend?" she moaned.

All the while calling the washer unladylike names, Jaime went back into her bedroom and gathered up her dirty clothes for a trip to the laundromat.

Her irritation only increased when a knock sounded at her front door.

"I don't need any company now," she wailed, throwing an armload of clothes on the bed.

She threw the door open, and her jaw dropped. Her visitor was the last person she wanted to see.

"Oh, it's you," she said rudely.

"I've had warmer greetings, but I guess that's doing pretty good for you." Mac stepped around her and entered the house. He turned and looked at Jaime dressed in a pair of faded jeans and a snug-fitting creamy yellow sweater. Her face was bare of makeup. His lips twitched at the change in his usually well-dressed accountant. "Why, Grandma, how you've changed," he chanted in a soft voice. "I think I like this image much better. You look more approachable."

"What do you want?" she demanded.

Mac's eyes swept over her, but the stormy expression on her face changed his suggestive reply. "I was in the neighborhood," he drawled.

"And the sun rises in the west," she blazed. "Look, my washer's on the fritz and I've got a lot of dirty laundry to take to the laundromat, so I don't have time to sit around and make small talk. I'm sorry if I'm being rude, but if you don't mind?" She looked at him pointedly.

"Why don't you have what's his name fix it?"

"Neil? He can't even turn a washer on much less fix one!" Her patience was wearing thin. "I don't need any bright and smiling faces today, so please go."

"What's wrong with your washer?" Mac asked crisply.

"How should I know?" She was exasperated by now that he wouldn't take her hints. "I'm not a plumber."

"Where is it?" He looked around until he found the open door to the laundry room and headed for it. With a minimum of effort, he moved the washer away from the wall and began inspecting the back. "I don't suppose you have any tools around here?"

"What are you doing?" Jaime had followed him and was instantly wary. She still remembered the time Neil had tried to fix her alarm clock. She ended up having to buy a new one.

Mac flashed her a wide grin. "I'm going to fix your washer,"

51

he informed her. "You're lucky that I keep a tool box in my truck." He ambled out of the room and out the front door.

Unable to believe his calm statement, Jaime could only watch him leave. He had just nonchalantly informed her he was going to fix her washing machine and didn't even wait for any response from her. He returned with his tool box and set it on the floor. He shed his black leather jacket and handed it to Jaime, then rolled up his shirt sleeves.

"I don't suppose you have any beer around here." He spoke absently, his attention already focused on the inner workings of the washer.

"Aren't you lucky that I do." Her sarcasm was evident as she turned to the refrigerator. "I use it for washing my hair." She opened a bottle and handed it to him.

He inspected the label and looked up. "Your hair has good taste."

An hour later, after a quick trip to the hardware store, Mac had Jaime's washer running.

"I don't suppose"—she tipped her head to one side, gazing at him thoughtfully—"that you know anything about garbage disposals?"

"Is this a test?" He grinned.

"No, mine's broken, and the price is right. A bottle of beer per job."

Mac walked over to the kitchen sink. "I'll have to raise my rates."

By midafternoon, Jaime was stunned as Mac also checked the seals on all the windows, fixed a warped door that stuck every time it rained, and put a new lock on the front door.

"I really don't know what to say besides thank you," she said gratefully, after he had put away his tools and washed his hands.

"You could feed me," he suggested. "I ate breakfast a long time ago and I'm a growing boy."

Jaime smiled at Mac's attempt to act the charmer. "A growing boy with a hearty appetite, I'm sure. I've got some beef stroganoff in the freezer that I can defrost in the microwave. How does that sound?"

"Fine." Mac followed her into the bright green-and-white kitchen and stood to one side, resting his hip against the counter. He watched her take a casserole dish out of the freezer and place it in the microwave oven. "Anything I can help you with?"

Jaime looked surprised by his offer. "Don't tell me that you can cook too?"

"Sure, a man can't eat in restaurants all the time. I can open a can with the best of them."

"Oh? You mean your little blond harem doesn't turn up on your doorstep to tempt you with hot meals?" she teased.

He flashed her a wicked grin. "No, I have a much better use for those little beauties."

Jaime grimly hefted a serving spoon, sorely tempted to hit Mac over the head with it. Instead she opened a cabinet door, took two plates out, and handed them to him. "Since you offered to help, you can set the table. The flatware's in that drawer over there."

Jaime quickly fixed buttered noodles and a green salad as the stroganoff heated. When she carried the food out to the table, she found Mac standing near her stereo inspecting her record collection.

"Very sophisticated taste," he commented, turning toward her.

"Not all of it." Why did he try to make her sound like some kind of blue blood?

"Enough." He held a Mozart concerto album in one hand, a thoughtful expression on his face.

"My mother bought most of those for me, saying it would help stimulate my mind. Rock music wasn't allowed in the house." Jaime set a bottle of wine on the table. "To her, the Beatles were bugs you found in the backyard."

"I bet you were prom queen too," Mac mused, rubbing his chin with his hand.

53

"And I bet your mother used to complain about all the girls calling you up on the phone," Jaime countered.

His face was expressionless. "Not me. My mother died when I was ten, and since no one knew who my father was, I was shuttled around in foster homes."

"I'm sorry," she whispered, appalled by this revelation.

"Don't be." His voice suddenly turned harsh, rejecting her sympathy. "I never was."

Not sure what to say, Jaime finally mumbled that the food was ready.

"I don't need your pity. That was a long time ago," Mac informed her in a rough voice.

Her head snapped up. "That's one thing you'd never need worry about with me," she retorted.

He studied her for a long moment. "Yes, I guess you're right."

Jaime could feel herself sinking into the dark eyes that now showed deep purple lights. She suddenly realized that it was intense emotion that caused Mac's eyes to seem purple. Most of the time they remained deep cobalt blue. She felt as if those eyes could see deep into her soul and she feared what he might find there.

"Eat before it gets cold," she ordered crisply, needing to break the eye contact between them.

"You're a good cook," he complimented her after he finished his second large helping of everything.

"Probably because I took home economics in school instead of mechanics," she said lightly, warmed by his sincere praise.

The conversation turned light and playful after that. Mac seemed at ease and almost eager to talk about himself. Jaime found out that he enjoyed playing touch football, jogged three times a week, liked country-and-western music and murder mystery films. In turn, he learned of her fondness for tennis, yoga, and musical comedies.

"For a feisty redhead, you have pretty tame tastes," Mac drawled, sitting back in his chair. "Or should I say boring?"

"If you're not careful, you'll find out just how feisty I can be," she retorted, rising to his bait.

His lazy grin was unnerving. "I never was into pain, but I think I could make an exception in your case."

"I'd be cautious if I were you," Jaime warned, standing up and piling the dishes on top of each other. "I haven't had my distemper shots yet."

"I'm not worried. I've got a strong constitution." He clearly was enjoying himself.

"I'm sure you do." She pursed her lips in thought, then stabbed where the male ego was the most delicate. "Although I understand that the approaching age of forty can be most trying for a man. It has something to do with midlife crisis." What was it about this man that encouraged her to say things she didn't mean?

Mac's eyes fired up. "I guess I'll just have to prove that point wrong, won't I?" he said genially, rising slowly to his feet with the lithe grace of a panther.

Jaime felt genuinely uneasy. Keeping wary eyes on him, she carefully set the plates down on the table and inched her way backward the way a small animal retreats from a cunning creature of prey. She didn't speak, not daring to break the thread of tension strung between them.

"You may be a sophisticated woman, Jaime Clarke, and have had all the benefits of an extensive education, but you still have a lot to learn about men." She dreaded this soft lion's growl more than his roar. It was much more deadly.

Mac reached out and gripped her wrist, pulling her toward him. "I've been haunted by the way you taste since that day I first kissed you," he growled, using his other hand to grasp her hip, keeping her body firmly pinned against him. "I mean to find out how accurate my memory is."

"No!" Jaime's protest was muffled by the swift descent of Mac's lips. Her brief attempt to free herself proved futile and she found herself defenseless against his plundering tongue. Her uplifted palm, meant to push him away, was imprisoned against his solid chest. No struggle was possible. Not with the iron strength holding her against his hard, warm male body. His virile desire was imprinted not only on her body but on her brain as well. The musky scent of his skin filled her nostrils, as potent as any strong alcohol, while a callused hand slid under her sweater and rested intimately against the sensitive skin of her stomach. The fingertips eased down until they reached the lacy border of her bikini panties, then beneath to feather lightly over the satiny skin, feeling the quiver of the taut muscles of her stomach.

A liquid heat flowed through Jaime's body. Moaning softly, she arched even closer against him until there was no space between them. Every hardening muscle of his body was branded on her skin. Her hands slid around the waistband of his jeans and up over the smooth skin of his back then down under the denim material to the soft cotton of his briefs. Wildly she wondered if they were the traditional white or some crazy color. Mac's hoarse words in her ear were enough to keep her fingertips mapping his skin. His tongue tasted then teased the interior of her ear, leaving her shivering and needing more of his touch.

"Touch me, Jaime," he rasped in her ear as he pulled one of her hands around to the front of his jeans. "God, I need you to touch me. Make it right for us."

The hardened flesh straining against the coarse denim material under her fingertips left her in no doubt where this was leading, and it stunned her for a moment. Groaning softly, she pulled away, turning her back to him. She wrapped her arms around her body, fighting tremors that had nothing to do with any chill.

Mac's hand lifted to grasp her shoulders and draw her back to him, but something stopped him at the last moment. Suddenly Jaime looked very vulnerable, and instinct told him he was in danger of frightening her off.

"Don't do this, Jaime," he pleaded softly. "You want me as much as I want you. Don't deny it. It could be so good between us. I know it."

"Please go." Her low voice throbbed in his ears.

"Jaime, I—" He broke off, frowning. How could he explain the fierce protectiveness he felt toward her? The urgent need to pick her up and carry her into the bedroom and make love to her? He wanted to take all the time in the world to make her his and never let her go. The thought of Neil doing just what he had been thinking of was enough to make his blood boil.

She shook her head, feeling the tidal wave of emotions ebb from her, leaving a dull ache behind. "Please, Mac." Her soft plea reached him more forcefully than any argument could. "I can't think right now. I need more time."

Jaime had never called him by his first name before, and the sound of it unaccountably filled him with hope. She was not indifferent to him; he knew that now and he also knew he could wait if he had to. He nodded slowly and turned away.

Mac was at the door before Jaime's low voice reached his ears. "Thank you for your help today."

The tone of her voice, suddenly so formal and impersonal, was maddening. "Sure, and thanks for the dinner." He paused and added deliberately, "Although dessert was a hell of a lot more interesting." The stiffness in her body told him his words had had the desired effect, but somehow it didn't make him feel any better.

Jaime closed her eyes. She could hear the front door close and the sound was enough to cut her in two.

This type of situation wasn't new to her. She had dated men who had accused her of being a tease, of leading them to a certain point then shutting them off with a single word or look. Their snide remarks hadn't bothered her before, because she had no feelings for them. Mac was different. He was nothing like the men she had known before. There was a raw virility about him that touched a nerve buried deep in her body. He had pulled away the covering on that nerve, exposing it, leaving her vulnerable to him. A dangerous situation.

Jaime's soulful mood didn't improve when she spent Sunday

57

afternoon at her mother's. Although she smiled and replied with the proper answers to Eileen's questions, her mind was clearly somewhere else. All afternoon long Jaime wished desperately that she were home. She needed all the time she could get to ready herself for work the next day, when she would have to come face to face with Mac.

CHAPTER FOUR

Much to Jaime's relief, Mac was out of the office a great deal during the following week. She wasn't sure how she could face him just yet. Not until she had time to rebuild and rearm her defenses.

Her week was busy as it was as she reviewed several more computer companies. One morning she had just seated herself at her desk when the phone rang. She barely picked up the receiver when a male voice vibrated in her ear.

"Get up here!" The line clicked dead.

"Yes, sir!" she muttered sarcastically.

Some perverse notion had Jaime stop for a cup of coffee and a lemon Danish that was reposing in a pastry box next to the coffeemaker.

"Didn't I hear the Man roar your name?" Sue asked, surprised to see Jaime slowly making her way to the stairs.

"I wanted to give him time to lower his blood pressure," she yawned.

"Better you than me." Sue shook her head at the other woman's foolhardy notion.

Jaime placed her napkin-covered Danish on top of her coffee cup and knocked lightly on the door.

It was obvious Mac hadn't cooled down one bit in the ten minutes since he had called downstairs.

"What the hell took you so long?" he demanded.

Jaime sat down in a nearby chair and took a bite out of her

Danish and a sip of her coffee before answering. "I didn't realize I was being clocked."

Mac's growl was unprintable. "I think we better talk about Ron Carlson," Mac said coldly, ignoring her flippant response.

Careful to show no reaction, Jaime leaned forward to carefully place her coffee cup and Danish on his desk. "I had assumed you had already talked to him before you hired me." It was difficult to pretend an indifference she didn't feel.

"I went by what I saw on your résumé and your letters of reference," he ground out. "I only talked to Personnel at Trenton. It seems someone over there just found out you're working here and thought I should learn a few choice facts about you." The dark expression on his face could only be construed as an inner force.

Jaime closed her eyes and drew a deep breath. "Yes, I can well imagine what they said." She spoke harshly. "All about my promotions by way of the controller's bedroom and I didn't know a debit from a credit but I certainly knew every position in the *Kama Sutra.*" Her eyes reflected dark storm clouds.

"Something like that, yes," Mac rapped out.

"Naturally." Jaime's voice dripped sarcasm. "I don't suppose you were told the reason that rumor began was because a few choice hints were planted in Ron's ear by someone outside the company. He then tried to maneuver me into his bed and I turned him down flat." She leaned forward in her chair, her clenched hands in her lap. "Of course, to make my point that I definitely didn't care for him as a lover I had to cast aspersions on his masculinity. That's when Ron decided it would be better to get rid of me before everyone found I had rejected him. His way was to make people believe I was the company hooker." Her body shook with suppressed fury.

Mac sat back in his chair listening quietly. The intensity of Jaime's reaction told him what he had wanted to know. There was no doubt in his mind now that she was telling the truth. He had never thought much of Ron Carlson before. Now he had no doubts on that score.

"Why did you allow him to run you out?" he said finally. "Your professional reputation could have been ruined just because of him."

Jaime smiled grimly. "Ron and I made a deal. I wouldn't accuse him of sexual harassment as long as he didn't tell any more fanciful stories." She rose to her feet. "Now what?"

Mac watched her with a hooded gaze. "When will you let me know about the different computer systems?"

Jaime caught herself before letting her mouth drop open. "You mean you don't want me to quit?" she couldn't resist asking.

"Do you want to?" he demanded tautly.

She slowly shook her head. For a brief moment, Mac's body relaxed and a faint smile touched his lips.

"Perhaps you'll do me a favor and some time you'll tell me exactly what you told Ron," he said quietly. "I'm sure your choice of words was less than ladylike."

A smile tugged at the corners of her mouth. "The air did turn a little blue," she murmured as she picked up her coffee cup and the remains of her Danish. "If there's nothing else, I'll get back to my office."

Mac watched her prepare to leave. "Jaime," he said softly, "I wanted to hear it from you. You understand what I'm saying, don't you?"

"Isn't it a shame that even in today's society, we're still guilty until we can prove our innocence." There was a hint of sadness in her voice. "I guess I should feel lucky that you believe me instead of Ron." She turned and walked out of the office, quietly closing the door after her.

Mac sat forward in his chair and slammed his fist down on the desk, swearing fiercely under his breath. If Ron Carlson knew what was good for him, he'd stay out of Mac's way for a long time.

When Jaime returned to her office, she glanced at Gina's empty desk then looked up at the clock to see that it was after ten.

"Carrie, has Gina called in?" she asked.

She shook her head. "Jaime, I'm getting worried. She's never been late like this before, at least not without calling first."

"If she doesn't come in here with a good reason, I'll be down on her so hard she won't know what hit her," Jaime stated grimly.

It wasn't too much later that Gina wandered through the front door with a dreamy smile on her lips.

"Where have you been?" Jaime demanded, almost past the point of anger.

"Hello, Jaime." She continued smiling, oblivious to her boss's temper.

"It's after ten and you didn't even call in to say you'd be late, Gina," Jaime ground out. "You better have a good explanation."

She patted Jaime's shoulder. "Alan proposed and I accepted," she said softly.

"What!" Sue shrieked, spinning around in her chair. "Oh, Gina, how fantastic!" She jumped up and ran over to hug the younger woman.

Jaime's anger instantly dissolved. "Congratulations," she said sincerely.

"We have to celebrate," Sue declared. "Gina, we're going to take you out tonight for one big bash and I don't want to hear any protests. Call Alan and tell him he better be prepared to share you for the evening."

"Sounds good to me, but he's on duty tonight and wouldn't be able to come," Gina replied. "He's a member of the California Highway Patrol," she explained to Jaime as an afterthought.

Jaime knew that if she didn't get their minds back on business right away, there would be little work done that day.

"I hate to be the bad guy, but do you think you can keep your head out of the clouds long enough to help the rest of us decide

62

which computer systems I'm to present to Mac?" Her smile took the sting out of her words.

"Sure." Gina beamed, then quickly apologized. "I'm sorry I didn't call, Jaime, but Alan proposed to me while we were having breakfast and we—" She blushed and Jaime immediately understood.

Despite Jaime's best efforts it took another fifteen minutes before Marie and Carrie were done squealing over their friend's good fortune. Finally they sat down to the business of deciding which computer systems to present to Mac.

"Kearny's the worst," Gina announced flatly. "With their system, we wouldn't be able to expand when we needed to and it didn't seem as if they lent that much software support. It would be as if once you had the equipment you'd be on your own."

"The rep was pretty cute though." Marie grinned.

"He may have looked good in a suit, but could his body have stood the test in a pair of tight jeans?" Jaime's dry comment drew amused laughter from her staff.

"Mac could pass that test with flying colors," Carrie threw in slyly.

"There are days when I get hot flashes just looking at him!" Marie laughed. "How about you, Jaime? How does Mac affect you?"

She smiled tightly. "I have enough to keep my mind occupied," she lied.

"Just wait until we go out tonight." Marie spoke up, all thoughts of computer systems suddenly forgotten. "This place is just crawling with gorgeous men!" Then, seeing Jaime's hesitant expression, she said, "Come on, Jaime, you have to go. After all, we're celebrating Gina's engagement."

She had been tempted to beg off this celebration, but then she'd have to spend the evening alone, since Neil was attending a conference in San Diego and would be gone for a few more days.

"Oh, I'll be going," she said with a laugh. Then, to change the subject, she added, "Now that we have our social schedule taken care of, shall we get back to these computer systems? What about Wilkinson? Their computer could easily be modified for future expansion." She consulted her notes on the pros and cons of the system.

When they entered the bar that night, Jaime was tempted to cover her ears. The band and the patrons seemed to be in some sort of competition to see who could make the most noise.

"Here we go." Marie led the way to an unoccupied table.

"Is there room for Sue and Ray too?" Carrie called out over the din of the music.

"Sure."

The waitress approached them for their order then slipped through the crowd with the ease of one who had been doing it for a long time.

"If we're lucky, we'll see her in a few years," Marie grumbled, watching the waitress stop at several more tables for orders.

"Not with Mr. Macho here!" a man's laughing voice announced. "The women just can't leave me alone. She'll be back in no time to gaze at my sexy body!"

The four women turned to greet Sue and her husband, a man of medium height with thick graying hair. He leaned over and planted a hearty kiss on Gina's mouth.

"Sorry it can't be more but my wife's watching," he told her in a stage whisper. "I just wanted to get that in before you become an old married lady."

When the drinks arrived, Jaime easily joined in the carefree banter as the group repeatedly toasted Gina's good fortune. Jaime found she was enjoying herself immensely and was happy to have made such good friends. But then suddenly a feeling of uneasiness came over her, some vague presentiment of danger.

She half turned, her expression frozen as she watched Mac fight the crowd to reach the table.

"Congratulations, glamour girl. He's a lucky guy," Mac greeted Gina, kissing her on the mouth. Then he immediately turned his eyes to Jaime, taking in her taut figure in her coffee-color silk blouse and cream-color pants.

With a sinking feeling, Jaime watched Mac squeeze into the only place left at the crowded table, the one directly next to her. It only made matters worse when she realized that her least movement caused her thigh to brush intimately against his.

Meanwhile, Mac sat quietly in his chair, unabashedly watching Jaime. He could feel his body tighten in response even though her smile wasn't directed at him. In fact, she seemed to be taking great care not to look directly at him at all and he didn't appreciate that in the least. He wasn't used to a woman having this explosive effect on him, and he certainly wasn't used to being so obviously ignored.

"Dance with me, Clarke," he leaned over to murmur in her ear, inhaling the subtle but potent scent of her perfume. With one hand braced on the back of her chair, he couldn't miss the tensing of her body.

"No, thank you," she said softly, carefully looking beyond him, as if keeping him out of her sight would make him disappear from the room.

"Yes, thank you," he mocked, unfolding himself from his chair and reaching down to pull her upright. He kept hold of her hand and practically dragged her onto the crowded dance floor.

"What makes you think I can dance?" Jaime challenged as Mac pulled her arms around his neck then settled his hands on her spine to keep her close against him.

"It doesn't take much imagination when I've seen you walk and move that enticing fanny." His breath was warm, his lips alarmingly close to her temple. "I'm sure you were put in dancing classes as soon as you could walk."

Stung, she tipped her head back. "Why do you resent me so much?"

Mac's large palm moved up to cup the back of her head and

65

press her face against his shoulder. "Honey, if there's one person I don't resent, it's you," he growled huskily, burying his lips in the fragrant cloud of auburn hair.

"I find that hard to believe." Her voice was muffled against the soft cotton of his shirt.

"Then start listening to your body instead of your brain." He moved erotically against her as the music began. People thought they had danced together for years, so fluidly did their bodies blend. This was more than dancing, this was the continuation of their love battle.

Jaime was pressed so close to Mac, she could smell the musky tang of his skin and see a faint sheen of perspiration on his forehead and upper lip. She could feel her nipples tighten against his shirt front, sending an intense heat through her lower body. She was acutely aware of every muscle in his body and of his hardening arousal. She had to get away from him before he learned how his touch was affecting her, but each time she tried to draw away, he pulled her firmly back into his embrace.

"Now, now, you're not one to create a scene, you know," he mocked her gently.

"There's always a first time." She tipped her head back, her eyes glittering under the overhead lights.

Jaime was relieved when the music finally stopped and she could safely pull away from Mac. With her head held high, she walked back to the table, painfully aware that all eyes were watching her with curiosity.

"I better be going," Jaime told them in a cool resemblance of her normal voice as she picked up her wool blazer from the back of her chair. "I'll see you all on Monday." She had to get out of there, and fast.

"I'll walk you out to your car," Mac offered instantly, resting his hand against the small of her back.

"I doubt anything will happen to me between here and the car," she snapped, then jumped as his hand lowered and pinched her painfully. She was tempted to turn around and slap his face, but as Mac had said, she disliked scenes. His eyes told her that he had correctly read her thoughts.

"Let Mac walk you out, Jaime." Sue spoke up, her face the picture of innocence. "You can't tell what could happen at night even around nice places like this."

Jaime was boiling inside as she left with Mac close behind. She walked rapidly once she was out of the crowded bar, but his long legs easily kept up with her.

"I don't need an escort," she informed him waspishly, digging through her purse for her keys. She stopped at the driver's side of her car and spun around to face him. "Fine, I'm at my car, I'm safe, and good night!"

Mac braced a hand against the top of the car on each side of her to prevent escape. "Are you safe?" he asked huskily, his eyes lowering to gauge the rapid rise and fall of her breasts under the thin silk of her blouse. "Did you feel safe out on the dance floor?" With each word, his body moved closer to hers, the gentle but suggestive thrust of his hips forcing her to feel the depth of his male heat. "Tell me, Jaime, do you feel safe now?"

She stared at the rugged planes of his face and experienced a choking sensation. "I'm never safe with you," she whispered, watching the purple overtake the dark blue in his eyes.

"That's where you're wrong," he breathed, leaning down to nibble her earlobe. "You've never been safer than when you're with me." His teeth grazed her jawline.

Jaime closed her eyes, trying to stifle the rocketing sensations in her body. Her breath came in short gasps as she licked suddenly dry lips. Slowly, inexorably, Mac slid his mouth over hers, his tongue probing, coaxing her response. A soft moan rose, unbidden, in her throat as her arms slid around his waist and her fingers dipped beneath the waistband of his jeans. She could feel her defenses slipping as his hand cupped her breast and molded the sensitive flesh to his palm. His thumb caressed the silk-covered nipple until a pulsating ache flowed through her body. Jaime was about to surrender completely and willingly to him when some voice of reason from deep inside her brought her back to her senses. She pulled away sharply, breathing deeply to dispel her arousal. Mac frowned, taking ragged breaths to restore his own equilibrium.

"What's wrong?" he demanded, moving to take her in his arms again, but this time she was able to resist him.

"Nothing," she replied tersely. "It's late and I have to go home." She then added in a deliberate tone, not taking her eyes from Mac's passion-etched features, "Neil's waiting for me."

His eyes narrowed, his nostrils flaring with anger. "So that's the way it is," he said slowly.

"Yes." She tossed her head back, barely managing to keep her features impassive. For now, she had to continue with this lie. May Neil forgive her for using him as a shield!

Mac lifted her wrist. His thumb absently rubbed the inner skin then threw it down as if the touch was distasteful.

"So be it," he snapped. "Good night, Jaime. Run home to your oh-so-proper lover. I just hope you won't get too bored."

It took all of her willpower not to run after him as she watched him walk back inside. To run after him and plead for the powerful possession of his mouth, of his body. Instead, she slowly got into her car and started the engine. She drove home more weary in mind than in body.

"Jaime, you're a fool," Neil informed her affectionately, several evenings later when she invited Karla and him for dinner.

She expelled a deep breath. She had told them about her working relationship with Mac and about his stopping by and staying to fix her washer. She made sure to omit the kiss, although Karla had glanced at her with quiet speculation, reading more into what she *hadn't* said.

"Why am I a fool?" she demanded, ladling creamy butter-filled oyster stew into three bowls. Karla carried them to the table, where Neil sat struggling with a reluctant wine bottle cork.

"Because of your feelings for your boss," he grunted, finally able to pull the cork free.

"Don't be silly," she scoffed, but not sounding too convincing.

"I think you've got the hots for the guy and just refuse to admit it."

Jaime's face turned a bright red at his mischievous and correct assumption.

"I'm right!" Neil crowed, pointing to her face. "You *do* have the hots for him, don't you?"

"Stop teasing Jaime, Neil," Karla ordered quietly. "You've been needling her about her boss all evening. If she decides to retaliate, I won't blame her or protect you."

"Good idea, since my mood is more suited to murder than passion right now," Jaime said between clenched teeth, glaring darkly at him.

"How does he feel about you?" Neil ignored her veiled threat, as he leaned his forearms on the table and waved his soup spoon about for emphasis. "I'm going to have to come by and see him for myself. It would be fascinating to find out what kind of man turns you on.

"How about lunch tomorrow?" he added, eyeing the large bowls of stew with a hungry leer.

"I'm on a diet," she quipped, sitting across from him.

"I like that!" Karla glared at Neil. "I'm lucky if you take me out for a hamburger!"

"Good, then I can have your mousse along with my own," Neil said, attacking his food enthusiastically.

"And he won't gain one blasted ounce either," Karla told Jaime with a groan. "While I'll be faithfully attending my exercise classes to make up for this sinfully delicious dinner." She turned to Neil. "And you behave or I'll leave the cooking to you for the next month."

"You can't threaten me like that." Neil laughed. "We both know you'd be afraid to eat anything I cooked." Much to Jaime's relief, he dropped the subject of Mac. Any reminder of her boss only served to jog her memory of that night in the parking lot, a night she was trying her best to forget.

A faint shiver ran through her body as she recalled the taste of bourbon on his tongue when he kissed her. It took a great deal of effort to keep her attention on the dinner conversation and most of the time she answered automatically, not seeing her guests' amusement at her absent air.

"I guess we better get going." Neil stood up and stretched his arms over his head. "Thanks for dinner. I'm glad to see you still remember how to cook." He dropped a light kiss on her nose. "Maybe if you wore tighter jeans, he'd notice you more," he suggested helpfully. "You've certainly got the figure for it."

"Neil!" Karla warned without effect. "Why I put up with you is beyond me."

"I'll see you later," he shouted as he was pushed out the door by a laughing Karla.

Jaime didn't think anything about Neil's casual "see you later" until the next day when Sue announced that Dr. Hamilton was waiting for her.

Jaime set her phone down, muttering under her breath, "I'll kill him for this."

"Hello, love," Neil said warmly, kissing her on the lips then stepping back to gaze appreciatively at her deep coral campshirt and tan pleated pants. "You didn't forget about our lunch date, did you?" he asked with a charming innocence that captivated even Sue.

"I'm sorry, I must have," Jaime said insincerely, while the expression in her eyes made dire promises.

"Sue—" Mac's entrance was abruptly halted as narrowed eyes took in Neil's hands on Jaime's shoulders.

"You must be Mr. MacMasters, Jaime's boss." Neil had now

70

draped a casual arm around her. "I'm Neil Hamilton." He extended his hand.

"Yes, I've heard about you." Mac smiled tightly, accepting the proffered hand.

"Hope you don't mind that I'm stealing your accountant for lunch." He grinned. "Don't worry, I promise to bring her back in a more amiable mood." He looked down at her stony features with a loving smile. "Go get your coat, sweetheart. I made reservations at our favorite place."

Not wanting to make a fuss in front of Mac and Sue—especially Mac—Jaime hurried away for her coat and purse. She didn't want to leave the two men alone for very long. When she returned, Neil was still talking in a friendly fashion to a stone-faced Mac.

"Same here, Nigel," Mac snapped, walking off and missing Jaime's furious glare.

"You really had to lay it on in there, didn't you?" she exploded, once they were inside Neil's car. "Of course, he isn't any better than you, deliberately calling you the wrong name. He knows what your name is!" At that moment, she wasn't sure whom she was angrier at.

"You sound as if he's done it before," Neil said as he accelerated the car onto the highway.

"Mac hasn't gotten your name right once," she said flatly. "I think he does it on purpose."

"Hm, it may not be deliberate," he commented. "Unconsciously he may prefer not remembering my name, therefore striking out my existence. I never realized I could be a threat to someone." He chuckled. "Maybe I should remind Karla what a menace to womankind I am. She might appreciate me more."

"You're beginning to sound just as conceited as he is," she retorted.

Jaime kept a cool silence during lunch while Neil rambled on about one of his students who had a crush on him.

"She even sprays perfume all over her papers," he told her. "And her handwriting is *very* sexy."

"I doubt Karla feels threatened."

Neil shook his head. "That man is *very* interested in you, Jaime. And I don't just mean your accounting abilities either. He looks at you the way a compulsive eater looks at a French bakery." He glanced down at his watch. "I've got a lecture in half an hour and you have to get back to work before your big bad wolf of a boss comes after you. Frankly, I wouldn't put it past him to do just that."

Jaime's mind catapulted back to the time Mac had taken her out to lunch. Biting her lower lip and trying to assume a composure she didn't feel, she reached for her purse.

Neil dropped her off in front of the building with a quick kiss. Just before he drove off, he leaned out of the car and with a devilish grin reminded her she didn't have too many good years left and she better snap him up while she had the chance.

Jaime's cross mood wasn't improved when she found Mac seated behind Sue's desk, the chair swiveled around so that he could easily search the contents of the nearby file cabinet.

"Enjoy your lunch?" he asked coolly, not bothering to look up.

For a moment, she stood fascinated by the play of the large, darkly tanned hands and was unaccountably fascinated by the sprinkling of black hairs on them.

Hearing nothing from Jaime, Mac turned his head and looked up. "You must not have had time to eat," he added snidely. "Your usual snappy patter is off balance."

"How did you know it was me?" she asked curiously, refusing to rise to his baiting. "There was no way you could have seen me come in."

Mac turned back to the file cabinet as if the contents interested him immensely. A long moment passed before he finally replied brusquely, "You wear a very distinctive perfume."

Jaime stared at him for a moment then turned away to walk to her office on shaky legs. Her eyes were clouded with thought as she mulled over Mac's reply. He had been able to know it was her by her perfume! She thought back to the scent of his cologne, a fresh spicy scent that was crisp and clean. Part of her acknowledged that she would be able to sense his presence in the same way.

CHAPTER FIVE

The next morning Mac stopped by Jaime's office just after she arrived for work.

"I'll be back a little before twelve to take you to lunch." He threw out his offhand invitation with casual aplomb. He didn't bother to ask if she had previous plans, just made his statement and disappeared from the doorway.

Jaime couldn't help but smile at the empty space where Mac had stood. She was getting used to his less than formal idea of asking for her company. Deep down she also had to admit she liked it.

"Hope you don't mind fast food today," Mac apologized, while putting the truck into gear. "I've got something to show you and it will be a little bit of a drive."

"I'm game for anything," Jaime said, resting her head against the back of the seat.

He shot her a wry glance. "Are you?" he murmured lazily.

She snapped her head around, but his features were as bland as if his question had no double meaning.

Lunch was hamburgers and french fries at a popular fast-food restaurant.

"You certainly weren't kidding about the fast-food part," Jaime teased as she dipped a crisp french fry in a small pool of catsup then popped it into her mouth.

"Be grateful that I'm feeding you first," he retorted.

After lunch, Mac ushered Jaime into the truck and got in

74

beside her. He was soon driving inland. She relaxed in the seat, knowing that questioning him would be pointless.

"What, no inquisition?" Mac raised his eyebrows in surprise. "Where's that feminine curiosity?"

"And give you the satisfaction of refusing to tell me? No thank you," Jaime said primly.

"I admit there's another way you could give me satisfaction." He kept his voice low, but he purposely meant for his words to carry to her ears. She ignored the hint.

It wasn't too much longer before Jaime recognized the prestigious community of Laguna Niguel. The homes there were large, well kept, and worth small fortunes. Mac's work-scarred pickup looked out of place there.

He turned up a narrow unpaved road that wasn't meant for public use and drove straight to the top of a hilly area. Finally, at the summit, he braked and stopped.

"Wow!" Jaime breathed, looking around as she stepped out of the truck. She turned around, appreciating the contrast between the green rolling hills on one side and the spectacular view of the blue ocean on the other. She held her arms out as if in praise.

"Can you imagine a house up here?" Mac's voice was hushed, in keeping with the mood surrounding them. "It would be almost all windows to catch the sun, a deck all along the second story, and a wrought-iron fence on the sea side so you wouldn't lose any of the view."

"Do you own this land?" Jaime turned back to face him.

He shook his head with a rueful grin on his lips. "Don't I wish. Actually, Royalton owns this whole parcel. Rumor has it that he wants to build six to eight custom homes up here with a good-sized plot of land adjoining each house. I'd estimate the asking price to be three to four million, rock bottom."

"I certainly hope that includes walls and indoor plumbing," she rejoined dryly. A thought came to mind. "You're hoping that if you get the contract for the condos, you'll have a good chance for this project too," she guessed.

Mac nodded slowly. "Think my ambitions are too high? Or am I just plain crazy?"

Jaime shook her head. "Only if you don't ask for one of the houses," she replied lightly. "Otherwise, I want first dibs."

He smiled. "Convince me," he coaxed silkily, holding out a hand.

Keeping in the spirit, Jaime grasped Mac's hand and pretended to go down on one knee. "Oh, please, Mister Mac," she pleaded in a high-pitched voice that bordered on a whine. "Give me a chance to leave the smog-infested city, a chance to get away from the bright lights and the fast lane of life."

He pulled her up and leaned back against the truck door keeping her in front of him.

"And what do I get?" he whispered, finding the delicate curve of her ear. His hands lowered to rest lightly on her hips.

Jaime drew a sharp breath. Funny, she never thought of the ear as an erotic spot until Mac had discovered it. "My heartfelt thanks," she managed to stammer out.

"Hmm, not good enough." Now his teeth were nibbling on her earlobe as if it were an exotic snack. His flexed fingers were splayed out over her hipbones as he pulled her closer to him, while he parted his legs, keeping her lower body cradled against his pelvis. "Try again."

"No," she breathed, knowing exactly what he wanted to hear. "This isn't for us, Mac." She had to keep lying to him as much as she did to herself. Why did he keep pushing her this way?

"Do you know what I dream of at night, Jaime, my love?" His husky voice vibrated against her skin.

She shook her head. She slid her arms around his waist and burrowed her face against his neck, inhaling the spicy scent of his cologne mixed with light perspiration. It was an all-male smell, one that both delighted and aroused her.

"I dream about making love to you. I can see you wearing a gown almost the same color as your hair." Jaime stiffened, thinking of the copper silk nightgown she had bought a few weeks before. There was no way he could have known about it! "You'll shine all golden fire in the moonlight, then I'll remove that gown." His hands moved over the shoulders of her lemon crepe blouse as if sliding straps down her arms. "Then the only silk I'll touch will be your skin."

Jaime closed her eyes under the spell of his words. Her breasts began to swell and the nipples peak. The denim-sheathed male fullness against her hips told her he was as aroused as she.

"Don't do this, Mac," she whispered huskily.

"After I finish kissing your bare shoulders and breasts, I'm going to mark every inch of your back with my lips, Jaime." His hoarse voice continued as if she hadn't spoken. "Then your stomach and breasts are going to receive some very special attention." His hand flattened over that area in a possessive gesture.

"M-a-c," Jaime moaned, unconsciously rotating her body against his palm.

"I'm going to enjoy tasting your body, Jaime, and making love to you." He cupped her buttocks, feeling the muscles tense in reaction. One hand slid around to the front zipper of her gray linen pants. His hand stroked the aching spot, increasing the sensual pain of his caress.

"No," she begged, shaking her head. She couldn't allow this to continue, but she was powerless to stop him.

He ground his hips against hers, and his tongue caressed the vulnerable areas of her throat until they seemed to burn under his sensual touch.

Her head was forced back under the impact of his kiss. There was no gentleness in the ravaging mouth as his tongue plundered the moist recesses of her mouth. Was she moaning or was it just in her mind? Her tongue searched out every crevice of the mouth dominating her and received a groan of satisfaction in response. Jaime thrust her hips against Mac's as he crushed her to his hard male body. Soon, she realized, there would be no turning back. It wasn't right! All he had to do was touch her and she went up

77

in flames. She knew she must break free now before it was too late. Mustering all her willpower, Jaime began to pull back.

"The time will come when I will find out all about you, Jaime," Mac promised in a raw voice. "Let me tell you how it will be for us. Deep and slow, as if we have all the time in the world." His low voice was an erotic growl as his lips found her shoulder under the notched collar of her blouse. "You're going to wrap your long and lovely legs around me and urge your own rhythm, but I'm not going to give in until you're ready to scream. Not until we've reached our limit. Not until I think I'm going to explode from the tightness and warmth of you, and then I'm going to push us both over the brink into oblivion. You've never experienced anything compared to our lovemaking, sweetheart. Every other man will be spoiled for you forever after our first time."

Mac's supreme arrogance was his undoing. Jaime's hands flattened against his chest and she pushed herself free of his grasp.

"It must be too much sun that has addled your brain," she said hoarsely, still trying to catch her breath. "What makes you think I'd ever sleep with you?"

He smiled, shaking his head as if listening to a fractious child. "Don't get yourself upset, Jaime," he soothed.

"*Upset!*" She took deep breaths to calm herself. "That's putting it mildly. I think we had better get back to the office." Her gray eyes flashed with anger.

Mac nodded, not offering any argument.

As they returned to the office, Jaime's mind raced. She was furious at Mac for his casual assumption that they would be lovers. What bothered her most, though, was that he was confident and sexy enough to make his prediction come true! If she didn't want his attentions, all she had to do was throw his employment contract in his face and walk out. That certainly was an easy choice.

* * *

78

The following Tuesday afternoon just after Jaime returned from lunch, Mac entered her office without knocking. Not bothering with a greeting, he settled in the chair across from her desk. He had stayed away from her since their confrontation the week before, as if knowing just how long to allow her to cool off. He was playing her with the skill of a well-seasoned deep-sea fisherman and the line was becoming tighter all the time.

"I'm afraid my report isn't ready yet," she murmured, wondering about the reason for his visit.

"That isn't why I'm here." Mac's eyes narrowed in concentration as he viewed Jaime's masked features. Every time he thought he had broken through her reserve, she threw up another wall. Well, there can only be so many obstacles before she runs out of them. "I just wanted you to know that I'll pick you up at seven for dinner."

Jaime frowned, annoyed at his high-handed assumption. "I don't believe I ever said I'd go out with you," she finally found her voice long enough to protest as she watched him rise from the chair and walk to the door.

With one hand on the doorknob, he turned back to her. His eyes danced with laughter as he replied, "Yes, you did." Then the door opened and he was gone.

For the balance of the day, Jaime knew all she had to do was pick up the phone and dial Mac's extension to tell him she wouldn't go out with him that evening. But she didn't.

That evening she searched her closet for just the right outfit to wear. It didn't take her long to find it.

If she expected to receive a reaction when she opened the front door, she was sorely disappointed. She could have worn a flour sack instead of her shimmering violet print skirt and matching long-sleeved sheer blouse. However, her own eyes widened in appreciation at the sight of a well-dressed Mac. In a pair of gray slacks and a white long-sleeved shirt open at the collar, he looked more handsome than she had ever seen him.

"Hm, I figured I'd be cooling my heels for at least an hour

79

while you finished getting ready," he commented, stepping inside.

"Not my style," she replied, reaching for her tan soft leather purse.

"You thought I'd drive you to dinner in my truck, didn't you?" he asked wryly, noting her startled reaction when he escorted her to a dark-blue Lincoln Continental.

"No, although I admit I didn't expect this." He settled her comfortably inside the car and slid behind the steering wheel. "I can understand why all the room though."

Mac laughed huskily. "I had a VW Bug once and I felt like a pretzel every time I got in it." He switched on the engine. "There's some tapes in that case there if you want some music."

Out of curiosity, Jaime inspected the assortment of cassette tapes. She wasn't surprised to find every country-and-western singer she had ever heard of represented in Mac's collection, and a few she hadn't.

"Of course, your taste may not run to knee-slappin', foot-stompin' music," he drawled, his voice remote.

Angry at Mac's automatic assumption of her tastes, Jaime selected a tape, slid it into the tape deck, and adjusted the volume.

"If we're going to do some character dissections, I think I should have a turn too. Let's see, where shall I start? You like country-and-western music, your steaks rare, baked potatoes with butter only, spicy hot chili; you think that jeans and boots are the only suitable attire; your women have to be soft, pliable, and not too bright, not to mention young and blond; you probably have season tickets for every sport in town; and beer is your favorite drink," she intoned loftily. "Did I miss anything?"

Mac's lips curved in a sardonic smile, his hands loosely clasping the steering wheel. "You're correct in everything but one. There are times when my favorite attire is a warm and willing woman," he said softly, watching her out of the corner of his eye.

Jaime turned her head and looked with a critical eye at Mac.

"I would say you might have better luck if you wore something at night," she commented lazily. "Dim lights wouldn't hurt either," she advised kindly.

"As I haven't had any complaints to date, I won't worry. Of course, if you'd like to find out for yourself . . ."

"Where are we going to dinner?" She had to change the subject before their conversation got out of hand. Mac was the undisputed expert when it came to sexual banter.

When he named a well-known Italian restaurant in northern Orange County, "What, no steak and potatoes?" slipped out before she could stop it.

"Not if I can have a good dish of lasagna instead."

Sensing the sarcastic bite in Mac's words, Jaime said softly, "I'm sorry, Mac, there was no reason for me to say that."

He silently considered her sincere words, then reached over, picked up her hand, and raised it to his lips. "Apology accepted," he murmured against her palm, the tip of his tongue tracing erotic lines on her skin.

A jolt of electricity shot through Jaime's body. She jerked her hand away and dropped it back into her lap. She felt her face redden as she heard his low, amused chuckle at her action.

"It's nice to know I can get under your skin," he told her. "Of course, I can think of more pleasurable ways of getting under that lovely flesh."

"I'm sure you can," she snapped. Was this how their evening would continue? If so, she was beginning to think she should have stayed home.

"I don't suppose you've ever been camping." Mac's voice broke the thick silence. Obviously he was going to be the one to initiate conversation. Although why he chose this particular subject was beyond her.

Jaime shook her head. "I'm sure you already knew my answer before I gave it."

"You should go. It's the closest to God a man can get." His tone was reverent, and even his face reflected a softness Jaime

81

had rarely seen. Instinctively Jaime knew the dark-lashed eyes would reflect a deep, clear blue now. "There's nothing like it. Crisp, cold air in the mornings that chases the cobwebs away, the heat of the midday while you're walking among the trees and watching the animals in their natural habitat, and the nights. . . ." He drew a deep breath. "Those are things you have to experience for yourself. And not in some vacation cabin either. You have to be out in the open to watch the stars come out late at night and hear the sounds of the night creatures. If you let yourself, you can feel as if you're a part of it."

A tingle ran down Jaime's spine at Mac's words and the picture he had painted for her. Funny, she hadn't thought he would have a romantic nature, but what he just told her said differently.

Further conversation was suspended as Mac slowed the car in front of the restaurant.

When they entered, Jaime was surprised by the spacious interior—a large formal dining room to one side and a dimly lit lounge on the other.

"Not like our chili dog hangout, is it?" Mac murmured out of the corner of his mouth, bringing a smile to her lips.

He stepped forward and gave his name to the headwaiter. Once again Jaime was struck by the air of authority Mac had.

Soon they were seated at a table and looking at menus. Jaime hardly glanced at hers before laying it down.

"I trust your judgment." She flashed him a smile.

Mac's stomach muscles contracted under the force of Jaime's smile. He always thought she was beautiful, but when she smiled like this, he wanted nothing more than to pick her up, carry her off somewhere, and lock the two of them away from the world. He wanted to explore every inch of her body with his hands and mouth, then start all over again. No other woman had affected him like this before. He had never wanted so desperately to give a woman pleasure, to satisfy her in every way possible. The blue in his eyes was gradually replaced by a deep purple as he stared intently at her face.

Jaime's smile wavered under the emotional signals Mac's eyes telegraphed to her. She lowered her head and nervously toyed with the silverware.

"Please don't, Mac," she whispered.

"Don't what?" he demanded roughly, feeling the tremors still rocking his body, tremors that began simply because she had smiled at him!

It took Jaime a few moments to formulate her answer. "Don't look at me the way you are right now."

"What way am I looking at you?" he pushed relentlessly.

Her eyes were flashing when she looked up. "You know very well what way." She was grateful for the interruption as the waitress arrived to take their order. She folded her hands in her lap and waited as Mac ordered for them both.

It only seemed moments after Mac had placed their order that their minestrone arrived, hot and properly spiced, served with warm, crusty bread and whipped garlic butter.

"Now I see why you enjoy coming here." Jaime eyed the large bowl of soup placed in front of her. "They serve your idea of good-sized portions. This is a meal in itself."

"Don't worry, you'll be able to eat every bite," he assured her.

During their meal, Mac threw casual questions at Jaime. He had an insatiable curiosity about her and was determined to learn all he could.

She told how her father had died the year before and how after thirty years of marriage and knowing nothing more than being a wife and mother, Eileen Clarke had no idea how to make her own way in the world. Now her life revolved around her daughter, her twice-weekly bridge club, and a few other social activities. Having been the head of a thriving small electronics firm that was run by a competent board, her father had left his family with more than adequate funds.

After dinner, Mac suggested crossing to the lounge to listen to the band. Jaime readily agreed. She felt a need to get up and move around. They found a table close to the dance floor. Mellowed from the rich food and wine, Jaime accepted Mac's invitation to dance. She knew the fast beat would guarantee that a distance would be kept, at least for a while.

When the music slowed to a popular love song, Mac merely moved forward and slid his arms around Jaime's waist. She had no choice but to settle her hands on his shoulders.

"Aren't you afraid I'll step on your toes?" She glanced at him provocatively.

"You didn't the last time." His lips lingered at her temple while his hands moved down over the base of her spine and upward to mold her hips closer to his.

Mac's warm, moist breath on her ear sent tingles along Jaime's spine. She tried to pull away from his close hold, but he merely tightened his grip.

He suggested hoarsely, "Just relax and enjoy. I sure intend to."

For a few magical moments, she did just that. Her body melted against his and her cheek rested against his shirt front. It was blissful. Mac's lips hovered over her temple, dotting tiny kisses dotted over her brow, then murmured unintelligible words in her ear. Muscular thighs brushed against soft ones, and their hips blended into motions of pure sensuality. His fingers insinuated themselves into the waistband of her skirt and under the silk of her camisole. Jaime shivered at the warm contact and knew if she didn't break away soon, she would be lost. Without a word, she pulled away and walked off the dance floor to their table, sitting down before she collapsed under the emotions he had aroused in her. Mac dropped into his chair and watched her with a broad grin on his face.

"Got to you again, didn't I?"

Silence.

"Talk to me, Jaime." There was a strange, intense note in Mac's voice.

"Why? We wouldn't agree anyway." She shrugged.

"I suppose you'd feel more at ease with Neville. His background must be a hell of a lot more blue-blooded than mine," he said harshly.

Jaime took a large swallow of her drink, feeling the alcohol take effect instantly. She sat in her chair, every line of her body rigid with anger. "The trouble with you is that you're a snob." Her soft voice cracked like a whip over his head. "You can't stomach the idea that someone might have had it a little easier in this world than you did and you condemn them for it."

His voice was equally cutting. "You're pretty free with your words, Clarke."

"Stop calling me that!" she hissed, leaning across the table so that she could be heard without raising her voice over the din of the band. "I'm not in the military and I'm not one of the boys."

Mac's eyes rested on the swell of Jaime's heaving breasts. "I'll vouch for that."

Incensed, Jaime picked up her drink and downed the contents in one swallow. "I'd like to go," she stated coldly.

Mac rose and walked around the table to Jaime's chair to pull it back. During the drive to Jaime's house, the air was thick with tension. She sat with hands clenched in her lap, convinced that when they reached her home, Mac would rudely push her out of the car and drive off. It wouldn't surprise her one bit if he did. No one talked to Mac the way she had and got away with it. She spared him a brief glance, but nothing in his manner betrayed any anger. If anything, he seemed totally relaxed.

Jaime gritted her teeth, wondering if she was strong enough to push him out of the car and drive it herself. A nice long walk certainly wouldn't hurt him one bit.

When they reached her house, Mac stopped the car and switched off the engine. He half turned in the seat, one arm resting along the back so that his hand was nestled against her shoulder.

"You have a very bad temper that should be controlled," he informed her.

"I should think you wouldn't want me around anymore then," she said stiffly.

Mac's body tensed. "Are you telling me that you're quitting?" he demanded.

Jaime turned a pair of startled eyes on him. "I was talking about after hours."

He shook his head, amazed that such a clear-thinking woman could act so erratic at times. "Let's go for a walk," he suggested, turning back and reaching for the door handle.

If anyone else had suggested going for a walk at such a late hour in the middle of winter, Jaime would have scornfully refused. Instead, she tightened the tie belt to her coat and waited as Mac reached in the back seat for his jacket and came around to open her door.

The wind whipped through Jaime's hair, sending stray curls across her cheeks. Her skirt molded itself to her thighs and legs.

"What exactly is the reason behind this?" she asked.

"I want to see if we can at least go for a walk without arguing."

Jaime frowned dubiously at Mac's idea but didn't voice her doubt out loud, knowing full well that would count as an argument. She stopped to take her shoes off before walking in the sand, and Mac slipped them into his jacket pocket. Immediately afterward she wished she had them back so she could make a quick escape. Why did he persist in wanting her company when all he did was goad her into a fight?

There were times when he appeared defensive about his background, and acted belligerent about hers. There wasn't a happy medium with them. She was so lost in her thoughts, she almost stumbled when Mac came to an abrupt halt. He reached out and took her hand in his, frowning at the chilled skin.

"Why didn't you tell me you were cold?" he chided. He tucked her hands in his coat pockets and slid his arms down her back.

86

His hands splayed out over her buttocks while his chin rested on the top of her head.

Jaime nuzzled her face against the hollow of Mac's shoulder. By barely turning her cheek, she could inhale the fresh scent of his cologne and feel the warmth of his skin. "It doesn't seem right, Mac," she mumbled against the soft material of his shirt. "Not after our fight tonight."

"This is very right," he contradicted gently. "Considering your perverse nature at times, you can be very relaxing when you want to be. As you are now."

"You're not exactly cool, calm, and collected yourself, you know," Jaime murmured, closing her eyes in contentment as she was enveloped by Mac's strong body. How could a man feel so comfortable?

Mac couldn't view Jaime in the same light. Not with her pliant body molded against his. Her perfume was more intoxicating than any alcohol or drug. He could feel her potency down to the pit of his stomach.

"Why don't we go back to your place?" he said huskily. Jaime could easily sense the direction of his thoughts in the vivid arousal of his tense body.

Jaime's teeth raked over her lower lip in indecision. She was sorely tempted to give in to Mac's unspoken suggestion, but she still felt uneasy about deepening their seesaw relationship.

"Are you sure it would be a good idea?" she asked softly, not wanting to come out with an outright refusal. For some reason her lips couldn't form the word no.

Mac took a deep breath before he released her, but he kept one of her hands warmly secured in his pocket. One arm circled her waist under her coat and pulled her to his side. "Personally, I think it would be an excellent idea," he replied seriously. Then he guided her back to the road and her house.

When Jaime unlocked her front door, Mac followed her inside. She had no time to switch on a light before he pulled her into his arms.

87

"Mac!" she protested, bracing her hands against his chest to give her some breathing room.

"Ssh." He dipped his head so that his tongue could find her ear. "You have to be careful in case there's burglars around."

Jaime could already feel herself weakening under the heat of Mac's moist caress. "Then"—she took a deep breath desperately trying to rebuild her defenses—"don't you think you should look around, just in case there is one?" Her hands slowly slid up to his shoulders and kneaded the broad outline.

"No way." His voice grew husky with arousal. "I need to stay here so you can protect me."

Her own voice was breathless from the feel of his warmth blending with hers. "Who's going to protect me, then?"

"Hmm." He appeared to give the matter great thought as his mouth created a burning path along the side of her throat. "I didn't think you needed any protection."

Jaime's eyes were closed and she was beginning to wish that this sensual upheaval wouldn't stop. She made no protest when Mac's hand inched its way under the waistband of her skirt, pulling the tail of her blouse out so that his hand could slide up over the silk of her camisole. Her own hands found his shirt buttons and were slowly unfastening them to seek the warm contours of his chest. Her nails lightly scratched the hair-roughened skin, feeling the muscles tense under her fingertips when she found his nipples nestled among the crisp hairs. She leaned forward and let the tip of her tongue taste the slightly salty texture of his skin. She paused a moment to nibble and slightly pull the tiny nipple with her teeth. Then she grew even bolder as her hand strayed down to his belt buckle, resting her fingertips against the cool metal, all the while sensing a vibrant heat so close. A heat that threatened to scorch her. How tempting it would be to test the power of that heat! To discover the molten inner workings of this man who could reduce her to flames by just looking at her.

Mac's animal growl echoed in her ear as he suddenly clasped

her about the waist and drew her up against him so that she could feel the intensity of his desire. Soon, all too soon, there would be no turning back for either of them.

"Jaime, you're driving me crazy," he gasped against her parted lips, grazing his teeth over her sensitive lower lip. "You're driving me insane and you enjoy it."

She took great gulps of air, inhaling the warm, musky scent of his skin. At that moment she wanted nothing more than to undress him and let him do the same to her. She wanted Mac, she wanted him badly. She couldn't deny it, not after that day on the hill. Her motions were slow and reluctant as she dropped her arms to her side and stepped back from his reach. Turning, she reached out for the light switch and flipped it on.

Mac's eyes were a deep purple, smoky with desire, and his chest heaved with ragged breaths. She doubted she looked any different.

"I'm not some little blonde who would willingly fall into bed at your slightest touch, Mac." She was finally able to regain use of her voice. "Oh, I realize that you see me as a challenge, but I'm afraid that this is one challenge you'll have to lose. You may as well give up now before the situation gets too sticky between us."

Mac's smile wasn't polite. In fact, it stung her in every raw nerve on her body. "It appears we both have a lot to learn about each other. You're a lovely lady and a very sexy one. I'd like you to know I don't usually do this sort of thing with my employees, but I felt you were special. I still do. I'm also a patient man and I can wait until the time is right. Good night, Jaime. Sleep well." His words sounded ironic.

It wasn't long before Jaime could hear the muted purr of the Lincoln's engine as it drove off.

Wearily she prepared for bed, all the time wishing she hadn't been so cold to Mac. She wanted him as her lover, but she didn't want the heartache that would inevitably follow. She had an idea that Mac enjoyed the attentions of women too much to ever think of staying with just one for any length of time.

She lay in bed as a dull ache stole over her body. It was the frustration that comes when your nerves are quivering for release but there is no one there to set you free.

CHAPTER SIX

Jaime was surprised by Mac's more than friendly attitude toward her the following week. She had assumed he'd ignore her completely after her abrupt rejection of him. She should have known better. Mac seemed to be enjoying this game of theirs. Deep down she knew he would win, but that didn't mean that she would make it easy for him!

Mac began stopping by her office almost every afternoon for a brief talk, so Jaime wasn't surprised the following Monday when he walked in. His first words, however, left her speechless.

He advanced toward her desk and leaned over to brace his palms on the polished wood. "Does Nigel know you want me?"

"There would be no reason for *Neil* to know any such thing, since it isn't true. Not to mention that he doesn't have a hold on me any more than you think you do," she snapped, her temper bristling at his domineering tone.

Mac's wolfish grin took her aback. "I'd like to have a hold on you, Jaime." His whispered words sent chills down her spine. "And I think you know just what kind of hold I'm talking about." He shifted until he rested his hip on the corner of the desk and could reach over to lightly rub his knuckles along her cheek. "I like to touch your skin and I know very well that you like me to," he murmured. "In fact, I'd like to touch you all over just to see if you're as soft in other places as you are here." His eyes lowered to run suggestively over the outline of her breasts.

Jaime jerked her head away. She experienced a burning sensation where his fingers had touched. "One thing I have to admit, Mac." Her voice sounded husky to her ears. "You certainly enjoy the cave-man approach to things, don't you?"

He continued grinning. "Ah, now, sweetheart, you wouldn't want me any other way."

Her eyes glittered when they met his teasing ones. "I wouldn't want you in any way, shape, or form," she announced softly but firmly.

Mac wasn't about to be put off. He noted the faint flush in her cheeks and her rapid breathing. Lowering his eyes, he could see her taut nipples straining against the soft wool of her sweater. He felt satisfied by her reaction.

"Never say something you can't back up with fact," he chided gently, sliding off the desk. "The signs are all there, Jaime." His eyes slid suggestively over the fullness of her breasts. "I better get some work done. It's good I have some physical work to do to keep my mind off my frustrations." He grinned at her as he left the office before she could throw something at him. Preferably something heavy as well as damaging to the ego!

Each day Jaime was finding it harder to continue their battle. Part of her feared that it wouldn't be long before she succumbed, while the other part was preparing to fight fiercely for her sanity.

When Jaime got ready to go out with Neil and Karla on Saturday night, her hands lingered over her violet skirt and blouse. Was she hoping to dispel the memories associated with the outfit by wearing it? Was it a trick of the senses or had the musky scent of Mac's cologne still clung to the fabric, even though it had just been dry-cleaned?

She brushed her hair until it gleamed, and added a touch of plum eye shadow along with dark mascara to play up her eyes.

"You look good enough to eat," Neil complimented her when he arrived at the front door.

"Do you ever compliment Karla?" Jaime asked him as he assisted her with her coat.

"Sure, the best way possible." He leered comically.

When they got to the car, Jaime groaned inwardly to see a man sitting there talking with Karla. Another of Neil's blind dates—and a complete surprise at that!

"I think I'll ask Karla if she would like to move in with me," she muttered under her breath.

"It's not what you think," Neil muttered back.

"Sure, it's not," Jaime replied cynically.

Patrick Hayward was blond, in his thirties, a good-looking associate of Neil's who had been teaching in Florida. He had come back to California for a leave of absence to write a book. At that moment he was staying with Neil and Karla until he could find a place of his own. By all rights, Jaime should be ashamed of her murderous thoughts about Neil, but she had been subjected to too many of his blind dates in the past. She merely gritted her teeth and quickly discovered that Patrick was pleasant and easy to talk to. But she silently admitted to herself that he was a far cry from Mac.

Dinner was delicious and the play that followed, lively. The evening was filled with bright conversation and laughter. So why did Jaime feel as if she would have been happier if she had stayed home? Her forced smiles and absent manner alerted Karla, but the other woman merely smiled slyly and made sure the men didn't notice Jaime's preoccupation.

When it was time to go home, she heaved a silent breath of relief.

"It was very nice to meet you, Patrick," she said cordially, holding out her hand when he escorted her to the front door. Luckily she didn't have to be rude and "neglect" to invite him inside for coffee.

"Perhaps we could go out without our chaperons one evening," he asked hopefully.

"Perhaps," she answered noncommittally. "Good night."

She unlocked her front door and stepped inside. Closing it

behind her, she expelled a weary sigh. All she wanted now was bed and sleep.

"It's about time you got home." She yelped in fright at the low-voiced growl that penetrated the room.

Jaime reached for the light switch and flipped it on. She found a scowling Mac seated in an easy chair with a drink in one hand. From his demeanor, she could guess that it wasn't his first.

"How did you get in here?" she demanded, tossing her purse on a nearby table and shrugging off her coat.

"I picked the lock."

She spun around. "You what!" Her eyes narrowed in suspicion. "Wait a minute, *you* were the one who installed a new lock on the door. You said it was the best around and next to impossible to pick," she accused.

"The front door, yes," he replied blandly. "The back door was a piece of cake." He glared darkly at her. "I'm surprised you didn't invite him in. Although it was better for him you didn't."

"At least he would have been here by my invitation. Not like you," she retorted, returning his dark scowl.

Mac settled back in the chair, looking the picture of animal comfort. "Why didn't you invite your new boyfriend in, Jaime? Don't tell me he's too much for you. Tell me something, did you decide I'm a better bet after all?"

"Don't be so cocky." She flushed when he smiled at her choice of words.

Mac set his glass down and got up from his chair. He walked over to Jaime, who had been watching his approach with wary eyes. When he reached her, he placed a hand against the wall on either side of her.

"The next time you decide to go out with any man, I won't just wait here for you, Jaime," he intoned dangerously. "The next time I'll come after you and rearrange his face. I won't even begin to say what will happen to you after I finish with him."

"Promises, promises," she mocked recklessly, defiance in every bone of her body. She'd be damned before she'd tell him her evening out was a party of four and her companion was far from the kind of man she'd like to date.

The glitter in Mac's eyes was her only warning before his mouth ground down over hers. Jaime's protest was muffled by his plundering tongue. His hard body pinned her against the wall, every taut muscle in intimate contact with her softness. Even a whisper couldn't have passed between them. Mac's hands reached down to grab Jaime's wrists and pin them against the wall at her shoulders. His leg insinuated itself between her thighs while his body ground and thrust at hers in a brutal parody of love.

Her eyes closed in humiliation at his cruel assault. Drawing on her last reserve of strength, she bit down on his lower lip. Mac's only reply was an animal snarl, and he pressed his mouth even closer until the taste of blood mingled with their kiss. When he finally drew back, his breathing was harsh and labored.

"Get out," Jaime whispered hoarsely, looking him straight in the eye.

Without a word, Mac turned and walked to the front door. Jaime waited until she heard his car drive away before she crumpled to a sobbing heap on the carpet. It was some time before she could rouse herself to get up and go into the bedroom. A look in the bathroom mirror revealed highly flushed cheeks on pale skin and swollen lips. She rubbed a first aid cream over the latter before she slowly undressed for bed.

Some hours later Jaime was still wide awake. She finally rose from her bed and pulled on a short robe. Her tumultuous evening was still too fresh in her mind for her to get any sleep.

Why had Mac acted the way he had? She could still feel the imprint of his body on hers but there was no revulsion in her thoughts, only wonder that she hadn't hit out at him before she ordered him to leave. Her fingertips massaged her temples in an attempt to banish the thoughts running through her mind.

Thoughts of Mac only confused her more. She felt as if she was beginning to crumble under the strain of it all.

Jaime paced around the dark living room in an attempt to tire herself out enough to sleep. Her head turned when the sound of the doorbell vibrated throughout the house. Giving no thought to the late hour, she walked to the door and opened it without bothering to find out who was there. She already knew.

Mac stood outside, his hands jammed inside his denim jacket.

"I couldn't sleep," he said simply.

"Neither could I." She stood aside to allow him to enter.

"You really should have a peephole installed. You didn't even ask who it was. I could have been anybody," he growled, closing the door behind him.

"I knew it was you." She faced him squarely, able to distinguish his features in the moonlit room.

Mac looked down and expelled a deep breath. "I have a horrible temper," he muttered, as if reluctant to reveal his faults.

Jaime smiled, knowing the courage it took for him to make that tiny admission. "I know," she said softly.

Mac's fingertips reached out and tentatively touched Jaime's still-swollen and bruised lips, which parted at his healing caress. His eyes roamed over the copper-colored silk nightgown molding her slender hips and thighs, then moved up to linger on her firm breasts.

"My God, Jaime." His voice was hoarse and he spoke with difficulty. His hand lowered and clenched at his side while his tense body looked as if he were afraid to move closer to her for fear of frightening or hurting her again. "I was right. I knew you would look this way. I don't know how I did, but I just did."

Jaime's hand crept up to her throat to combat the suffocating feeling threatening to overtake her. Was that why she had worn this gown? Had she somehow known he would come back? How could a man, merely by the expression in his eyes, send a liquid heat coursing through her veins? His eyes were riveted to her lace-covered breasts, and she could feel them swell in memory of his heated touch, the nipples taut with longing for that caress again. Nervously she slid her tongue over her dry lips, pulling Mac's eyes to the provocative gesture.

"Jaime!" His low rasping groan sent waves of desire through her body.

"Please don't do this, Mac," she whispered, drawing the edges of her robe protectively across her body. "I can't understand what you're doing to me. You anger me, you—"

"Arouse you?" His murmur hung in the air unanswered. "Tempt you? Force you to realize the urges of your body?" He stepped forward, taking her in his arms. "Do you know I lie awake at night dreaming of you looking like this for me?" he said, burying his face against the hollow of her shoulder and inhaling the soft fragrance of her skin. "Lord, if I'm dreaming this time, please don't wake me up."

Jaime's arms slowly lifted and encircled his neck. She rested her cheek against his chest, listening to the uneven thumping of his heart. One arm lowered, pausing to unfasten one button on his shirt, then another, then a third. She turned her face and kissed the warm skin, the pelt of dark hair a sensuous pillow for her face. She wasn't surprised to feel him trembling in her arms, trembling nearly as much as she was.

"You taste like salt," she whispered, as her tongue caressed the hair-roughened skin of his chest.

Groaning, Mac lifted his head while his hands grasped Jaime's face and raised it to his. His kiss was so fierce and hungry that her mind reeled under the impact. His tongue entered her mouth with none of the anger of before, only a passion that couldn't be denied. The tip explored and darted to each corner, curling around hers in a moist love play, only to stroke and taste the honey of her mouth. His body moved closer to hers until his hands slid down to circle back to grip her buttocks and press her against his hard-muscled body.

"You're so damn beautiful." His hot, moist breath seared her mouth. "In that nightgown and with your hair tousled, you look like a fire-haired sorceress."

Jaime could feel the passion running through Mac's body, through the tense muscles of his chest, the taut thighs, the pulsating masculinity, although he kept it under tight control. His fingers tangled themselves in her hair and his thumbs probed the corners of her mouth, letting her taste the now-familiar flavor of his skin.

"Oh, Mac, what's happening to us?" she breathed, grazing her teeth over his thumb, keeping her gleaming eyes on the darkened features.

"Something that's been building up since that first day, something you've always tried to deny—until now. Well, you can't deny me any longer." His mouth lowered to cover hers again.

His hand wandered down Jaime's throat until it slid under the lace neckline of her nightgown and found the swelling flesh that silently cried out for his touch. His thumb and forefinger rolled the nipple, teasing it into a soft rose-tipped pebble. Jaime's whimpering moan, drawn up from the depths of her throat, was swallowed by his ravaging kiss. She slid her arms around him, her fingers delighting in the strong muscles of his back. The soft, sensuous silk of her gown whispered against the rough fabric of his shirt and jeans, as their bodies pressed ever closer together.

Mac's ragged breathing was harsh as he lowered his hands to cup her buttocks and press her up into the cradle of his hips, forcing her to recognize his thrusting force.

Jaime inhaled sharply as he swung her up in his arms. Her own arms automatically circled his neck for balance. "I'm too heavy," she murmured faintly even as she nuzzled his throat with her lips. She was caught up in a madness she didn't want to end.

"I'm not your puny-muscled boyfriend, Jaime," he informed her, walking in the direction of her bedroom. He carefully laid her down among the tumbled covers as if she were a fragile work of art.

Jaime propped herself up on one elbow as Mac shed his clothes with unhurried ease. There was no embarrassment in her eyes as she watched. "You're beautiful," she whispered, afraid any louder sound would disturb the magical mood surrounding them.

Mac smiled as he stretched out beside her. "I've dreamed of this moment, Jaime," he said in a husky voice filled with desire. His hand was gentle as he explored each curve of her body, memorizing it by his touch.

She looked up, awed by the reverence he paid her, oblivious to all but his sensual touch. She had never felt more alive.

Mac pulled off her robe, then drew her nightgown over her head, stopping to kiss each spot the soft material uncovered. He then drew her against his heated body.

"How can any woman be so beautiful?" he rasped, tracing the delicate lines of her collarbone with his fingers, moving slowly down to her breasts then lower across her stomach and lower still, satisfied to find that her arousal was building as rapidly as his.

Matching him in this game of seduction, Jaime slid one silky leg over Mac's leg, rubbing up and down, reaching a higher point on his thigh each time.

His passion bordered on tender violence as he alternately nipped and licked along her throat and up to her earlobe, deliberately keeping away from her moist parted lips that begged to be possessed.

"Mac," she pleaded, digging her nails into his hips and undulating under his hardened body.

Muted whimpers of joy erupted from her throat as his mouth swooped down over hers, his tongue thrusting and parrying with hers. She arched her body, her hands moving feverishly over the perspiration-slick skin of his back, the fingertips pressing against his spine even as her hips writhed in sensual motions under him.

"So sweet," he muttered thickly, his mouth trailing a searing path down to her breast, his teeth seducing a turgid nipple. When he finished with one, he moved to the other, sending shafts of pleasurable pain through her body to meet at that secret center that cried out for fulfillment even as his hand slid up her inner thigh on its silken journey.

"You have burned me, witch," he growled seductively, moving over her to part her thighs with his knee. "You've left scars that can never be healed."

"Mac, please." There was no shame in her plea as she moved against him and reached down for his throbbing heat.

His other leg slid between hers as he prepared to release her frustration. His hands slid under her buttocks to raise her to him.

"Jaime?" he questioned softly, needing to know that she wanted him as badly as he wanted her. She arched up, rotating her hips against his in a seductive motion. It was all he needed.

Jaime's cry of passion was swallowed by the force of Mac's kiss at the same time she was consumed by his thrusting body. For a moment he became still, whispering words of love, but she wouldn't allow it. She wanted more and her body encouraged him into the rhythm they had been fated to follow from the beginning. She became unaware of everything but the force of his body against hers. His tongue darted in her ear as he hoarsely muttered praises of her beauty, her body, and her femininity. She could feel an unbearable tension building up in her body as she strained to reach heights she had never explored before.

"Give in, Jaime. Give in! It's yours for the taking," Mac rasped, his breathing harsh in her ear.

She strained further, her cries mingling with his hoarse murmurs. In one shattering instant she plunged into a deep, dark abyss. Only the knowledge of Mac's arms holding her kept the fear away.

Sometime later, Jaime lay wide awake in Mac's arms while he slept deeply. Her body felt a little sore yet languorous even as her mind raced madly. She had never experienced such abandon in a man's arms before. She had lost all control and it frightened her. She wanted to dismiss this as a midnight madness, but she couldn't. Mac was right, this was the result of a sexual tension that had been building up between them for a long time. But what would happen now?

Carefully edging out from under the heavy weight of his arm, Jaime crept out of bed and walked over to the window. She was so lost in thought that she wasn't aware of the night air chilling her naked body. In fact, she was so engrossed she didn't stir when a blanket was draped over her shoulders and wrapped tightly around her.

"That's a good way to catch a chill." Mac's breath was warm in her ear.

"I didn't notice the cold." Jaime didn't turn her head to acknowledge him.

His lips feathered over her temple. "You're so beautiful." His raw voice was barely audible.

She didn't move. She didn't know what to say. How did you tell a man that he had been the most passionate, exciting lover you had ever met and that you were afraid of what he could do to you?

He sighed deeply, drawing a ragged breath before speaking. "I knew it would be this way with us."

Nothing.

Mac swore under his breath and questioned her in a rough voice. "Talk to me, Jaime."

There was no need for lies now. "I was afraid."

"Afraid?" He was incredulous. "Afraid of what?"

"You."

"You were afraid of me?" He closed his eyes and shook his head. "What did I ever do to frighten you?"

"I was afraid of this happening. I knew it would be like this, an explosion. I just hadn't realized it would be of this magnitude." There, she had said it, pure and simple.

Mac's fingers edged under the blanket and reached for her bare shoulders in a butterfly caress. Unable to restrict himself to so simple an act, he finally pulled her tightly against him.

"Oh, Jaime!" he groaned, burying his face against her neck.

101

"At least you're being honest with me. Is that how you felt? I only know that I feel as if I had died and been reborn at the same moment. This never happened to me before and I know it hasn't for you either."

Jaime circled her arms around his waist, resting her cheek against the mat of dark hair on his chest. "I'm so confused," she whispered shakily. "You're right, Mac. But it was even more than that. You were so caring and gentle. That counts just as much as, if not more than, the passion between two people." She couldn't bring herself to say that she loved him yet. That would be final, irrevocable step, and she wasn't prepared to take it yet.

He gripped her chin and jerked it upward. "Then let's find out more about that spark of passion between us," he rasped, his eyes filled with dark fires. He picked her up and carried her back to the bed. The blanket soon slid to the carpet.

A gasp caught in her throat as he intimately caressed the inside of her thighs. "Why are you doing this?" she asked.

Mac drew his head back just enough to see her face. "Because you bring me to life." His fingers gently traced the shape of her bruised lips, then his mouth followed that same path down to the swollen shape of her breasts and over the smooth surface of her stomach. His tongue darted into her navel, tantalizing her before moving further down.

Jaime closed her eyes as the swirling mists engulfed her in a haze of sensuality that promised never to end.

CHAPTER SEVEN

Jaime awoke slowly from a deep slumber. She raised her head barely an inch from her pillow and looked around with drowsy eyes. She had been sleeping on her stomach with her face buried in the pillow. The room felt very strange; something was different.

"Good morning, sleepyhead."

Her head swiveled around on the pillow. Mac stood in the doorway of the bathroom dressed only in his jeans.

"You were sleeping so soundly, I didn't want to disturb you." He grinned. "Hope you don't mind that I used your shower."

She rolled over and started to sit up until she remembered she was naked. She knew it was silly to act so modestly, but still she kept herself carefully covered by the sheet. "No, of course not," she murmured, still half asleep. "What time is it?"

Mac walked over, retrieved his shirt from the floor where he had dropped it the night before, and slipped it on. "About ten." He sat on the edge of the bed and took her slightly chilled hands between his own, rubbing them briskly to warm them. "By the way, I also took the liberty of checking the contents of your kitchen. You don't have much in the way of breakfast makings. What would you say to going out for all the pancakes you can eat?"

Jaime groaned. "I'll go for something a lot lighter and plenty of coffee."

"Deal." He grinned. "You're not much of a morning person, are you?"

"You're right." She returned his smile all the while hoping he would pull her into his arms and recreate the magic of the night before. Instead, she took the initiative and looped her arms around his neck, resting her face against his throat.

"Hold me, Mac," she whispered. "Please just hold me for a minute so I won't feel like a one-night stand."

At her words, his arms wound tightly around her. "You're far from that, my love. I can see I'm going to have to change your way of thinking," he murmured, then offered quietly, "Look, the least I can do is run home, shave, and change. Why don't I come back in about forty-five minutes and we'll go out to breakfast. Will that give you enough time?" He gently pulled her head back and brushed his lips lightly across her forehead.

"More than enough time," she said softly.

It wasn't until then that she realized he had been holding his breath as if afraid she'd refuse. "I'll see you later." He stood up and walked out of the room.

A few moments later Jaime could hear the sound of the front door closing and the hum of Mac's car as it started up.

In the shower, Jaime thought back over the previous night. Somehow none of it had been a surprise. It had all been ordained, just as Mac had told her. He had arrived on her doorstep in the middle of the night to apologize for his show of temper and within a matter of minutes they were making love. She wasn't sure who she had learned more about in the past few hours, Mac or herself.

It didn't take her long to shampoo, blow dry, and style her hair, then dress in gray pants and a light-blue long-sleeved sweater with a matching plaid shirt underneath, the pointed collar neatly aligned over the V-neckline of her sweater.

When Mac arrived, he was wearing a pair of designer jeans and a cream-colored fishermen's knit sweater, looking all too masculine for Jaime's peace of mind. He took her hand as they walked to the car and she could feel the electric current pass between them.

This was a man she could count on in so many ways. Mac was a considerate lover, taking her own desires into account before worrying about his own fulfillment. She had never been so attracted to any man before, yet there were so many conflicting feelings running through her mind!

As the car sped down the highway, Jaime carefully slid across the seat until her thigh touched Mac's. He didn't acknowledge her action, but a tiny smile appeared at the corners of his mouth.

The drive was made in silence, but Jaime could sense every movement of Mac's body as he drove.

"Where are you kidnapping me to, sir?" She affected a haughty English accent.

He glanced down, flashing a wide grin. "If I had my way, it wouldn't be to breakfast." One hand left the steering wheel briefly to caress her cheek with his knuckles.

She returned his smile. "Too bad," she replied airily. "Too bad, because I've decided that I'm starving and I intend to order the biggest breakfast I can find on the menu."

"This I'll have to see to believe," he teased back.

The restaurant was bright and airy, specializing in any type of omelet imaginable. Their table was colorful and situated in a corner away from most of the crowd.

As Jaime sat there, she didn't realize that her face held a warm, contented glow. A glow many of the men noticed when she crossed the dining room.

As Mac watched Jaime drink her coffee, he wanted nothing more than to drag her away and find the wanton and passionate woman he had unleashed the night before. There were faint shadows under her eyes but she was more beautiful than before, if that was possible. That gut-wrenching desire flared up in him again when Jaime glanced up and smiled.

"You're staring at me as if I have two noses," she said lightly, hoping to break the sensual web woven around them.

105

"You amaze me." He shook his head and smiled. "I wonder how many sides there are to your personality and how long it will take me to learn them all."

Jaime returned his smile and looked down to where Mac's hand covered hers on top of the table. "I think you've discovered more than enough," she said softly.

No, I haven't, he wanted to tell her. I want to know everything about you, to become a part of every intimate detail of your life. However much he wanted to tell her this, he didn't. He wasn't going to frighten her any more if he could help it and the words he wanted to speak could do just that. How could he hope to explain his feelings when he himself didn't understand them completely. Mac had felt possessive about Jaime before, but now! Now he felt as if he would guard her with his life. She had given him her passion and he had given her his heart. He wanted to say these words out loud, but he knew now wasn't the time.

Their conversation turned lighter as they continued to eat, and soon they were laughing and joking together. Jaime enjoyed Mac's mild teasing and the bites they shared from each other's plates.

"Lady, if you don't remove your hand from my thigh, we may have to stay here a little longer until I can become decent again," Mac whispered wickedly in Jaime's ear, then roared with laughter at her red face.

"You have a dirty mind, MacMasters," she retorted, her lips curving in a broad smile.

"No, just one track." He grinned, leaning over to drop a brief kiss on her nose, not caring who saw.

When they left the restaurant, Mac's guiding hand rested against the small of Jaime's back. It was a possessive gesture that two people didn't miss as they rose from their own table to leave.

"I suppose I have to take you straight home," Mac teased, as he unlocked the car door.

"Fancy meeting you here!"

Mac's body stiffened at the sound of Neil's jovial voice and the

106

word muttered under his breath was far from polite. He spun around with Jaime beside him, to confront Neil and a companion.

"Do I rate an introduction?" Karla asked brightly, linking her arm through Neil's. She hadn't missed the murderous lights in Mac's eyes.

"Karla Fields, John MacMasters, my boss." Jaime knew her ruse was now over. Now to see how Mac would handle this piece of news. "Karla is Neil's, uh"—she paused delicately—"roommate."

The red flush along Mac's cheekbones told her he understood her meaning.

"I'm pleased to meet you, Mr. MacMasters," Karla said serenely, holding out a hand, which he reluctantly took. "Jaime has spoken of you often."

He shot the redhead a chilling glance. "I'd love to know what she said," he said, irritation lacing his voice.

"Nothing like a Sunday morning breakfast out, is there?" Neil asked cheerfully.

"Where's your house guest?" Jaime asked, wishing Mac would loosen the tight grip on her hand before he broke some bones.

"Apartment hunting," Karla replied. "Patrick discovered that our sofa bed isn't all that comfortable." She flashed a smile in Mac's direction. "Something we took into consideration when we bought it. The next time we all go out for dinner, you'll have to come with us, Mr. MacMasters." Then she added slyly, "I'm sure Jaime would have enjoyed herself more Saturday evening."

This time Mac's eyes seemed to bore through Jaime's skin. "If you'll excuse us, we have to be going," he muttered. "Jaime and I have a few things to discuss."

"I'm sure you do," Neil murmured, exchanging a smile with Karla. It hadn't taken him long to read the questions in Mac's eyes. Jaime was going to have a lot of explaining to do!

Mac roughly pushed a now-wary Jaime into the car and

walked around to the driver's side. His hands clenched the steering wheel so tightly, his knuckles were white as he accelerated down the road. She wasn't sure what frightened her more, the forbidding expression on his face or the excessive speed with which he took the sharp curves.

"Mac, please slow down," she begged, digging her fingers into the armrest, fearing they would veer off the road at any moment.

Without answering, he turned off the road and stopped the car. He half turned in his seat and reached out to grasp her chin in an ironlike grasp.

"Let's talk, Jaime," he said in a dangerously silky voice, his eyes hard as stone.

"About what?" She winced as his fingers tightened their grip.

"Neil Hamilton!" he spat out the name. "You said that he was your lover!"

"No, I never said that," she replied carefully, mindful of the raging temper just lying beneath the surface.

"All right, then you deliberately allowed me to believe that he was," Mac roared. "It must be an interesting threesome, although Karla doesn't look like the kind of woman who would care to share her man."

"I needed the protection!" Jaime shouted back. "I was afraid of what you were doing to me and I thought that if you thought he was my lover you'd keep away from me. Neil's only a good friend."

He turned away and draped his arms over the steering wheel, staring out through the windshield. It hurt like hell that she had gone to such lengths to try to keep him away from her. How could she think of such a stunt? The only way he wouldn't have touched her was if she had been married and even then, it would have been next to impossible at times. "What happens now that I know the truth?" he asked bleakly. "Tell me something, were you ever going to let me know, or were you going to let the thought of him sharing your bed eat me alive for a while longer?"

Jaime hesitantly reached over and stroked his cheek, willing the tension to leave his body. "It's all a part of something new," she whispered. "I think it's something we've both got to learn about each other—trust."

Mac closed his eyes and turned his face so that his lips could caress her fingertips. What was it about this woman that could inflame him just by her touch? Even now, with his temper still simmering, he wanted her. Last night hadn't been enough to satisfy him. He could still remember the feel of her skin under his touch, the way she tasted, how she would cry and whimper as he drew her into his power. The tight muscles of his body screamed for him to take her now, but a saner part knew this wasn't the time.

"Was he ever more than just a friend?" He had to speak to keep things on a sane level even if he might not like the answer. Deep down, after seeing them together, he doubted that they had ever been lovers, but he needed to hear it from her. He needed reassurance.

Jaime's fingertips caressed his lips. "I've known Neil since I was six. He's like an older brother, and the only woman for him is Karla." She suddenly began to laugh. "Do you realize that you've finally gotten his name right? Is it because you've finally discovered he isn't a threat to you?" she teased.

"Don't push me," he warned darkly, although the look on his face told her more than enough.

Mac put the car in gear and turned it back onto the road. This time, his arm rested along the back of the seat behind Jaime as he drove. He hated to admit how much he needed the woman beside him. He knew he would soon have to find a cure for his craving before it destroyed them both.

When they reached Jaime's house, Mac walked her to the door but made no move to enter.

"Thank you for breakfast." She managed a bright smile, although her body was quivering with reaction and, perhaps, anticipation.

Mac recognized her caution and hated himself for instilling it in her. "I've got a ton of paperwork to catch up on, I should be going." He followed her lead. "I'll see you tomorrow." He made no move to touch her before turning and walking back to his car.

Jaime waited until the car was speeding down the road before walking inside. She hated to admit how empty she felt now that Mac was gone.

Monday morning, Jaime dressed with great care. She had spent most of the night before lying awake in bed, thinking of Mac; but she wasn't about to let him know he could cause her to spend a sleepless night.

"How was your weekend?" Sue asked, greeting her as she entered the building.

"Always too short," Jaime answered with a shrug, halting at Sue's desk for a moment.

"What, no handsome man to brighten it up?" she teased.

Jaime smiled faintly, thinking of Mac. "I should be so lucky." She yelped as a hard palm firmly connected with her backside then lingered against the firm, rounded skin for a moment in a caress.

"Be in my office at ten, Clarke, so we can discuss those computer systems you're so hot about," Mac said crisply as he headed for the stairs.

Sue's eyes were full of speculation when she glanced up at a red-faced Jaime. "My, my, isn't the boss becoming a little too familiar with the hired help nowadays!" she teased. She hadn't missed Mac's brief caress when he had passed by Jaime.

"It's a good way for him to shorten his life span," she grumbled, resisting the urge to rub the smarting area. "If I'm going to meet with his highness at ten, I better get a few things out of the way first."

The first part of the morning passed quickly, and promptly at ten, Jaime climbed the stairs to Mac's office.

He was in his favorite position, with his chair tipped back and his booted feet propped up on his desk. Several file folders holding Jaime's reports on the various computer systems lay on the desk's polished surface.

"I've already confessed that I don't know a damn thing about computers," he admitted. "While your reports are very thorough, I still feel pretty much in the dark. Which do you feel is our best bet?"

"Harrison Electronics," Jaime replied without hesitation. "They have an excellent track record of keeping their clients informed on any new versions of their software. Each of the girls will have to attend classes for about a week, but if we do it on a rotation basis, we shouldn't have any problems."

Mac lifted his feet off the desk and sat forward, leafing through the folder Jaime had mentioned. He grimaced as he glanced over one of the pages.

"It's also one of the most expensive," he pointed out.

"Not in the long run."

He shook his head and looked up with a faint smile on his lips. "Expensive wench, aren't you?" His eyes roamed boldly over her smoky-topaz silk shirt and cream-colored pleated wool pants. Some people might wonder why someone with her ability was willing to bury herself there, but he was glad that she did. "What are you doing for lunch?" he asked huskily.

"Having lunch with the boss," Jaime drawled, lights dancing in her eyes. Whatever had been bothering Mac yesterday had now disappeared and she was glad. "At a very quiet and exclusive hideaway that serves the best chili dogs in town."

"You've got great taste, Clarke." The fires in his eyes belied the brusque voice. "Or is your choice of restaurants due to the fact that you're taking me to the cleaners for a computer?"

"You won't be sorry, Mac," she assured him.

"Then you better call Harrison Electronics while you've still got me softened up and before I change my mind. I'll be by for you about twelve thirty."

Jaime nodded as she pushed herself from her chair. "Oh, I

talked to Jack Howard's office and gave them the plumbing specs for their bid on the Royalton job."

"Did you explain about those special specs?"

A ghost of a smile curved her lips. "Naturally, the sunken bathtub with Jacuzzi, all the mirrors and fancy hardware. I wouldn't be surprised if the model units have round beds with a fur bedspread and fancy bar in the living room, if not in the bedroom too."

"Hm, might be a good investment." He rubbed his jaw reflectively and gave her a wicked smile.

"Now you're definitely talking about breaking the bank," she laughed. "See you at twelve thirty."

It didn't take long for office gossip to circulate about the budding romance between Jaime and Mac.

Now when they went out to lunch, they sat on the same side of the booth, Mac's thigh warmly pressing against Jaime's. Although he still spent most of his time away from the office, he usually managed to be back around lunchtime.

As the bid day approached, tension grew in the small building. Mac spent more time in his upstairs office, poring over blueprints and scribbling figures on sheets of paper that were then given to Sue to decipher and type up for inclusion in Jaime's part of the bid proposal.

Late one afternoon Jaime was working feverishly, not pausing to even consider how many rolls of calculator tape she had gone through. She looked up with a frown at the sound of her door opening. Mac entered and sat down in the chair directly across from her desk.

"Frowns leave lines, you know," he informed her blandly.

"And bosses who walk in on their extremely busy employees make it difficult for them to get their work done," she retorted.

Mac shook his head, grinning broadly. "I can tell you're not in the best of moods today. No matter, I'll be out of your hair in a minute. I just wanted to see if you've got everything pretty well ready for tomorrow."

She nodded. "As ready as we'll ever be."

He hesitated for a moment. "Do you think we've got a good chance?" he asked quietly.

Jaime looked at Mac, aware how concerned he must be if he was coming to her for reassurance. In the past few weeks she had discovered just how much this project meant to him. It was what Mac had been working toward all these years. The coup of taking this bid from all the larger firms that would be bidding on it would mean that he'd never lack for work. She only wondered if Frederick Royalton knew how much he would be getting if Mac won the bid.

"The champagne better be properly chilled for tomorrow night's celebration," she informed him softly.

Mac hauled himself out of his chair and walked around to the desk pulling Jaime from her chair and into his arms. "Woman, you're better than any of those false words of encouragement," he murmured, bringing his mouth scant inches from hers. Then his lips finally descended on her waiting ones.

His kiss was leisurely, as if he had all the time in the world to taste and explore her mouth. Jaime's lips automatically parted when the tip of his tongue touched her, sliding into the dark caverns of her mouth. A raw groan erupted from his throat as he pulled her even closer toward him. She could feel his potent arousal through the thin wool of her pants and writhed expectantly against him.

At that moment Jaime couldn't have cared less where they were, as long as Mac kept kissing her the way he was. That was all that mattered. She clasped her hands about his neck and thrust her fingers into the dark silk of his hair.

Mac's thigh had situated itself between her legs, pressing against her, tormenting her. Jaime's soft moan was proof enough of her arousal. Reluctantly he released her with a lingering caress to her buttocks.

"Sorry I don't have time for more, darlin', but I've got to go," he said with a sigh as he straightened up.

Jaime stared at him, her eyes a misty gray, full of desire. "Come again?" She was still finding it hard to concentrate after the lusty kiss he had just given her.

Mac glanced down at the clock on Jaime's desk. "I hadn't even meant to stay this long, but there's just something about you that drives me crazy." He leered playfully.

She took a deep breath. "Are you trying to tell me that you're going out tonight while the rest of us stay here and slave away on the final preparations for this bid?" There was the faintest hint of anger in her question.

"'Fraid so." He absently patted his back pocket as if to reassure himself he hadn't forgotten his wallet. "See you in the morning." He lightly kissed her lips before walking to the door.

"How nice," Jaime drawled icily. "The boss goes home to relax and his employees stay behind to do the dirty work." She refused to admit that jealousy motivated her anger. Although they saw each other a great deal during the day, Mac hadn't made any suggestions about going out in the evenings, leaving her a little puzzled and hurt by his casual indifference. She was almost beginning to wonder if he had found himself another woman with whom to indulge his nighttime pleasure, someone who might prove more satisfying than she had. That thought was rapidly turning into an open wound.

There was a strange quiet about him. "The last word I would use to describe you is one of my employees, Jaime," he said quietly. "I'll see you in the morning." He opened the door and left.

Jaime dropped back into her chair and took her fit of temper out on her calculator while calling Mac uncomplimentary names under her breath. She refused to remember the times he had worked late and the many more hours he put in on this project. Instead all she remembered was his calmly informing her he was leaving early when he knew she still had several hours of work ahead of her.

Several hours later Jaime realized that one set of figures she needed was missing. Finally she remembered that Mac had taken them earlier that day. She only hoped she could find them in the jumble of papers that always cluttered his desk.

It took her a good twenty minutes before she found the sheets on Mac's drafting table. As Jaime turned away, the cover of a book caught her eye and she walked over to inspect it closer. She picked the book up and read the title. It was a textbook on small business management. Jaime slowly opened it and found Mac's name written on the flyleaf. Inspecting it further, she found his dark scrawl scattered among the pages. She carefully replaced it so no one would know she had looked through it. There were a great deal of questions she wanted answered and, at the moment, only one person could help her.

Sue was also working late. Jaime found her typing busily, and even at this distance, she could tell the older woman wasn't working on a set of figures. She quietly approached the secretary and stood close enough to read the typed paper.

"Business law," she read out loud.

Sue stopped typing and spun around in her chair. "I didn't hear you!" she gasped. "That's a good way to scare a body to death." She effectively blocked Jaime's view of the paper. "I'm typing up one of my son's papers for him."

"I didn't know your son was named John MacMasters." Jaime smiled thinly. "Is that why Mac left early tonight? Because he had a class?" she continued. "He's taking night classes, isn't he? That's why there's some evenings we haven't been able to get hold of him."

Sue nodded reluctantly. "Three nights a week," she explained. "He's been working to get his degree in business administration."

"Funny that he never mentioned it to me," Jaime replied.

"And here I've been thinking that he's been out with one of his little playmates."

Sue easily recognized the hurt in the younger woman's voice, as well as the hint of insecurity. With each passing day, she was tempted to shake these two up and lock them in a room until they had talked things over. She remembered Mac's vehement instructions not to say a word to Jaime about his classes.

"It hasn't been easy for him," Sue told her. "Working the long hours he does here and going to school in the evenings."

"How long has he been going?"

"Almost two years now." She gestured toward the typewriter. "I feel as if I'm learning right along with him. He may be able to put a building up in no time, but he sure can't type, so I decided to put him out of his misery and volunteered to type up his reports for him."

"Why didn't he ever mention this to me?" Jaime asked, hurt that Mac had left her in the dark about something that was obviously very important to him.

"I think he was afraid to," Sue said gently, going on to explain. "It hasn't been easy for him to return to school, and I think he feels that you might try to patronize him, since you already have your degree."

Jaime shook her head; for some reason she wanted to laugh. Why did people always think things came easy for her? Did she make them see it that way? "It doesn't make any difference," she replied huskily. "Oh, I admit I was lucky enough not to have to work while I was in school, but I carried an extra heavy load and there were times when I wondered if I'd ever learn it all. It's not what you learn in school that counts, but what you learn out here in the real world." She waved her hand in a circle for emphasis.

Sue looked worried. "Are you going to tell him you know?"

Jaime smiled tightly, still feeling the hurt at not being let in on something so important to Mac. "No, it's all your and Mac's deep, dark mystery." She paused, looking down at the sheaf of

116

papers in her hand. "I'm pretty tired. I think I'll finish these at home."

The secretary looked at her closely. "You're taking this personally, Jaime, and you shouldn't," she guessed shrewdly.

"You're right," she admitted softly, smiling at Sue's perception. "I guess it's just a shock when you think you know a person and then you come to find out you don't. Don't worry," she assured the older woman. "I won't give Mac any cause to be suspicious. This is just something new for me to assimilate." She turned to head back to her office for her purse and coat. After wishing Sue good night, she left the building.

Jaime still wasn't entirely sure why it bothered her that Mac hadn't told her about his attending school. She couldn't imagine that he was ashamed of it. If anything, he should be proud of his accomplishments and not care who knew it. There, that was what bothered her: his not telling her.

Now she knew at last why his evenings never seemed to be free. She would gladly have offered to help him in his studies. But perhaps he didn't want her help. Did he really think that she would lord her so-called knowledge over him? If so, then he didn't know her as well as he thought he knew her.

Jaime didn't get to bed until past two o'clock that night, and the headache she felt coming wasn't going to help her concentration the next day. She was beginning to wish she hadn't bothered to go up to Mac's office for those figures. Had they been that important or had she been meant to find that textbook? She'd never know.

Jaime rose at her usual hour, feeling as if she hadn't slept at all, which was closer to the truth than she wanted to admit. It didn't help her mood any to see the dense fog rolling past her window. She quickly dressed and left for work, not any happier to discover her car was low on gas. A quick stop at the gas station to fill up the Porsche and then it was a slow crawl down the highway to the office.

She'd have to be very careful. Her car blended in much too well with the fog and she had to be on the watch for cars coming up too fast on her tail. Due to the less than favorable conditions, she was forty-five minutes late, even though she had purposely left the house a half hour early.

The moment she entered the office, Mac came racing downstairs. "Where the hell have you been?" he growled.

After almost being rear-ended on the highway twice, Jaime's mood wasn't the most amiable. "Having breakfast with Robert Redford," she growled back, striding toward her office.

"I'm not in the mood for your snappy patter today, Clarke," Mac snarled, staying close on her heels. "Do you realize how many accidents have occurred on the highway this morning?"

"I saw three and was almost in two myself, is that enough?" She entered her office and hung her coat up. "Let's see, that makes five, doesn't it?"

The red on Mac's face was enough warning that his temper was beginning to boil over. "You could have called that you were going to be late."

"That's pretty difficult when I left early," she retorted, throwing her purse on her desk. "Now, if you'll excuse me, I have some work to do." Her eyes flashed. "I do believe this is the day you submit the bid on the Royalton project?"

"Right," he growled, walking out and slamming the door behind him.

A few moments later Gina entered cautiously. "I figured it was safe to come in since Mac had left," she explained. "He's been going crazy for the past half hour and was about ready to go out and look for you."

"Look for me? Why?" Jaime was mystified. Dense fog was a common enough occurrence in the beach areas during the winter.

Gina smiled with a knowledge of a woman beyond her years. "I think he was afraid you had been in an accident."

118

"You sure wouldn't have known he was worried by the way he chewed into me when I came in," Jaime said angrily.

"That's men for you. They always seem to yell at us when they're really grateful that we're safe." The younger woman laughed. "Alan does that all the time. When I'm late, he's angry because I'm late but he's happy that I'm all right. There's no pleasing them."

"Amen to that," Jaime said fervently.

"I'd say you need a cup of coffee," Gina volunteered. "Sue brought in donuts. You want one?"

"Two." She managed to smile. "Perhaps you should use one of the coffee decanters. I have an idea I won't be getting out of here too much today."

Gina nodded and left.

Jaime collapsed in her chair and rubbed her temples with her fingertips. Her headache was worsening. She could see the wisdom in Gina's words, because all the time Mac was yelling at her, she couldn't miss the look of relief in his eyes. She only wished he had taken her into his arms instead. It would have been more satisfying after her traumatic morning on the road.

CHAPTER EIGHT

The day was as hectic as Jaime had expected. As a general contractor, Mac would oversee the construction of the building. In bidding for the job, he needed estimates from all the subcontractors who would be involved. MacMasters Construction had invited these subcontractors to submit their own bids for their part of the project. Since there were many possible subcontractors for each category, Mac would then sit down with Jaime, go over the figures, decide which would be the lowest and in their best interests, and add it to their growing total. At the end of the day, Mac would send his sealed bid by messenger to Royalton Properties office. Hopefully, within the hour, they would know if he had submitted the lowest bid and won the job.

Jaime hadn't been too sure how Mac would treat her after their argument that morning, but his manner toward her was polite and there was a faint teasing in his voice as if her cool, unapproachable attitude amused him.

They sent out for lunch, and the small group shared a large pizza in Mac's office while answering telephones and marking the bids.

Jaime was amazed at how easily everyone worked with each other during this high-pressure day. While she had worked on bids before, in a large company she never had the feeling of truly helping. Here the air of group accomplishment was strong.

By six o'clock Jaime wasn't sure if she ever wanted to see another telephone again. She relayed her thoughts to the others as they sat around Mac's office waiting for the results of the bidding. Tension was high, but everyone carefully ignored their innermost fears and chattered happily.

"A woman without a telephone?" Mac teased softly. "You'd go crazy before the day was out."

"Uh huh." She shook her head. "Right now I wouldn't want to see two tin cans and a string!"

Then the phone rang. They all froze, and Mac hesitated before reaching for it slowly. Everyone waited expectantly as he spoke. He gave away nothing by his words or actions, and for a moment Jaime was afraid that perhaps they hadn't done well enough. Mac hung up the phone and looked at each member of his staff.

"Well, I guess the easy work is out of the way," he said quietly. "Now all we have to do is build ourselves a condominium complex."

Ray, who had showed up to help with the phones, gave out a whoop and hugged Sue tightly while everyone else talked excitedly.

"I have some champagne in the refrigerator downstairs." Mac looked directly at Jaime. "How about helping me? I believe we have some celebrating to do."

She smiled widely and nodded. Right now she'd do anything he'd ask her to do.

They were silent as they walked downstairs to the small kitchen. Mac motioned toward a bag that held plastic wineglasses and opened the refrigerator door to pull out two bottles of champagne.

"First things first," he told her, drawing Jaime into his arms.

Jaime's arms automatically linked around his neck. "Congratulations, boss," she murmured, taking over. She pulled his head down for her kiss and circled his mouth with the tip of her tongue, pausing first to tease the corners of his lips. The tension in his body told her the effect her moist kisses were having on him, but she wasn't about to stop or let him turn the tables. This was her way of letting him know how happy she was for him.

121

Two buttons of his shirt were unfastened and one of her hands slid inside to trace the muscular contours of his chest.

"Jaime," Mac groaned, pulling his head away and resting his chin against her forehead. His breathing was hard and labored from her blatant attempt at seduction. "Damn, this isn't exactly the place for a hot and heavy necking session."

Her soft laughter rippled through her body. "And just when I was getting into it too," she mourned.

He locked his hands at the base of her spine and drew back slightly, regarding her with suspicious eyes. "I'd sure be interested to know where you picked up some of those handy household hints."

"Hmm." She continued caressing his chest. "Oh, here and there."

"Such as?" he demanded.

"Such as—" Jaime leaned forward to kiss the rapidly beating pulse point in his throat. "This very sexy man named John MacMasters who has seduction down to a fine art."

The sigh of relief was expelled audibly. "You little witch." He chuckled. "Come on, we better get this champagne upstairs before they send a search party out for us and get the shock of their lives."

Jaime smiled, remembering the glances she and Mac received when they left the office each day at lunchtime. "I don't think anyone would be too shocked. They would just wonder why we hadn't locked the door."

He shook his head in amazement. "I'm beginning to think I have a staff of sex maniacs here with you as the head maniac. Cut that out, Jaime!" he ordered her as he felt his buttocks patted by a very feminine hand.

"I just wanted to see what it would be like," she said airily, picking up the bag that held the glasses. "After all, you do it to me, so it's only fair I get a chance to do it to you."

Mac herded her out of the kitchen. "Fine, then join me for

dinner and you can try out anything your little heart desires," he suggested huskily.

"All right." She smiled back.

"Hey, you two, what are you doing down there, growing the grapes for the champagne?" Ray's voice called down the stairs, with Sue's voice, chiding her husband, clearly heard in the background.

"What did I tell you," Mac murmured. "People would think we can't be trusted alone."

"They could be right," Jaime said cheekily, hurrying up the stairs.

After the champagne was finished and congratulations given out all around, the group slowly filtered out of the office after Mac's heartfelt thank you to his crew.

"I couldn't have done it without you," he said sincerely.

"Does this mean we get a raise?" Carrie spoke up.

"How about my letting you come to work a half hour later tomorrow?" He grinned.

"Take it," Gina advised. "Otherwise he might take it back."

Fifteen minutes later Mac locked up the building and guided Jaime out to his car.

"Perhaps I should just follow you to the restaurant," she suggested.

Mac shook his head. "Your car will be all right here," he told her as he unlocked the passenger door and ushered her inside.

Jaime huddled inside her coat until the heater began to warm the car's interior.

"I'm glad for you, Mac," she said honestly, turning her head to look at his profile. A sight she knew she'd never get tired of. "You really deserve this."

He smiled and reached out for her hand, pressing it against his thigh. "It's the biggest project I've ever taken on, and truthfully, I'm a little scared," he confessed. "Something like this could make me or break me."

"I'd go with the former, then," she said confidently.

123

Mac drove up the coast to Balboa Island, heading for a popular restaurant that specialized in spaghetti.

When they sat at the table, Jaime felt relaxed and happy to be sharing this time with Mac.

"Between the champagne we had earlier and this"—Jaime gestured toward her filled wineglass—"I don't know if I dare drive home."

"No problem," he assured her. "I'll drive you home. Your car will be safe overnight."

Jaime rested her elbow on the table, chin propped in one hand. "What, no designs on my body?" she teased, knowing she was flirting with him and enjoying it.

"Oh, sure," Mac drawled, deciding to join her game. "I have plenty of designs I'd like to try out." His eyes centered on the low-cut V neckline of her lavender silk blouse.

"And you accuse *us* of being the sex maniacs!" She wrinkled her nose at him, laughing and loving his suggestive comments.

During dinner, Jaime was tempted a few times to ask Mac about his classes but was afraid she might ruin the spell that had been woven over them. All she could do was sit back and hope he would soon feel confident enough to tell her.

"Let's go for a walk," he suggested as they left the restaurant. Not wanting the evening to end, Jaime eagerly accepted.

They walked down toward the pier and along the dark beach front with its many T-shirt shops, roller skate rental shops, bathing suit shops, and its usual assortment of bars. Mac had kept Jaime's hand warmly clasped in his, stuffed inside his jacket pocket for extra warmth.

"I used to spend a lot of time around here," he commented casually.

"Doing what?" she asked idly.

"Getting into trouble. Half of the Newport Beach Police Department knew me by name." Now there was a harshness in his voice that hadn't been there before and Jaime wanted nothing more than to erase it.

"When I was in high school, I used to come down here with my girl friends to meet some boys," she said lightly, striving to break his moodiness. "When you're sixteen and trying to act eighteen, it can be pretty hard. We'd wear our best bikinis and drape ourselves out on the sand watching the boys play volleyball or body surf, all the while hoping they were watching us too."

"I'm sure they were watching you." Without warning, Mac pulled Jaime into a dark corner between two buildings, his mouth easily finding hers. There was no gentleness, only a roughness of the heart as he drew her tightly against him. Jaime could only slide her arms around his middle, melting under his burning kiss and searching tongue. She could feel the cold concrete of the building at her back as Mac pressed her none too gently against the wall, but it didn't matter. All that mattered now was the warmth invading her body from his. They were totally oblivious to their surroundings. At that moment Jaime wouldn't have cared if Mac had pulled her down to the ground and made love to her right there. His roughness was exciting to her in a way she hadn't experienced before and left her only wanting more of him. A discreet-sounding cough suddenly brought them back to the present. Mac kept Jaime's hot cheek against his shirt front as they turned to face a uniformed policeman.

"You folks should be ashamed of yourself," the policeman said. "Don't you think you're giving the kids around here a bad example?" He squinted and looked closer. "Mac?"

Mac stepped forward to take a better look. "Harry?" He whooped with laughter. "It *is* you!"

"I should have known." The gray-haired man chuckled, accepting Mac's outstretched hand. "I have to admit I've missed finding you in these dark corners these past years."

"Please, you'll ruin my reputation." Mac grinned, looking at Jaime's still-red face. "Harry is one of the Newport Beach's finest who used to know me in the old days," he explained. "Just don't listen to any of his stories, because I'd never be able to live them down."

"Oh, you're doing all right for yourself," the policeman assured him. "I saw that write-up on you in one of the local magazines. You've done well for yourself and I'm proud of you." He went on to tell Jaime, "There were some who figured he'd end up in San Quentin, but I knew he had more brains than that. This boy's a hard worker. All he needed was for somebody to give him a chance." He grinned broadly. "We used to find him necking with one of his girl friends in these dark alleys or parked up on the bluffs. It looks like he hasn't changed there."

"I doubt he's changed in a lot of areas," Jaime commented dryly, looking up at Mac's reddened face.

"I guess I better get the lady home," Mac cut in. "It's good to see you again, Harry." He shook the other man's hand.

"I'm just glad to see your taste in ladies has improved." He winked. "Now the two of you get on before half the teenage population around here starts copying you. I've got enough to do as it is."

Jaime remained silent during the short walk back to the car. Mac decided that anything he might say at that moment might go against him. It hadn't taken Jaime long to figure out what Mac had been like as a young man in his teens and she sincerely doubted that any girl could refuse him anything. He would have been rebellious, angry at the world, and even then, sexy as hell! In other words, a loaded keg of dynamite, and any girl would have been the match to light the fuse.

Mac switched on the car heater not long after he turned on the engine in order to allow the interior to get warm. Jaime sat back in her seat staring straight ahead, but as she thought back to the scene at the beach, her sense of humor took over. First a faint smile appeared on her lips. As the situation replayed itself in her mind, she began to laugh, first softly, then louder.

"What do you think is so funny?" Mac growled, turning his head in her direction.

"Us," she replied, still laughing, her shoulders shaking with mirth. "If you stop and think about it, it is pretty funny. From what that officer said, it's been almost twenty years since you've been caught in the middle of a hot and heavy necking session. At least your taste has improved," she teased. "Sometime, you'll have to tell me about some of your old girlfriends. Were they blond too?"

Mac gave her a look that could kill. "Now I know why I stayed away from redheads," he informed her gruffly, putting the car in gear.

Jaime was still chuckling to herself as they pulled up in front of her house.

"Is that where you would have taken me on a date if I had known you then?" she asked him.

"You would have still been in grade school," he growled, escorting her to the front door.

"I always was very precocious for my age," Jaime said flippantly. "Always went for older men too."

"You're really pushing your luck," Mac warned darkly.

"I'm not the one who ran into someone who knew you during your 'bad boy' days." She unlocked her front door and walked in with Mac following her closely.

"Ten years ago your mother wouldn't have allowed me within ten feet of you," he said roughly, pulling her coat off and throwing it on a nearby chair. He grasped her arms, spun her around, and pulled her against his chest. As before, his kiss sent primitive flashes through her body. Jaime moaned softly and melted against his body, sliding her hands under the waistband of his slacks. "Ten years ago I wouldn't have known what to do with a stormy-eyed witch like you the way I do now," he rasped.

Jaime tipped her head back and looked up at him. "What would you do now?" she purred, enjoying the power she had over him.

"This." There was no time for her to take a breath when his mouth captured hers. No time to gain hold of her senses as his hands roamed freely over her body, finding every pleasure point.

She arched her body into his, fervently wishing there wasn't a barrier of clothing between them. Soon all that could be heard was his labored breathing and the soft moans torn from her throat. She uttered a faint cry of dismay when Mac slowly disengaged himself from her arms.

"Don't go," she pleaded huskily, not caring how she sounded. All she knew was that she wanted him . . . badly.

He shook his head. "Sorry, sweetheart, but for once I'm going to show you I can be a gentleman and leave you somewhat untouched," he told her.

"But I don't want to be untouched!" Jaime protested, then reddened as she realized how her words sounded.

Mac laughed and pressed an all too brief kiss on her lips. "Don't worry, I'm going to be hurting just as much as you are," he informed her. "Humor me."

Jaime looked up at him and knew that he spoke the truth. What they had started had only whetted their appetite for each other. The last thing she wanted him to do that night was act the gentleman. "Mac, was it because of meeting that policeman?" she asked him.

He smiled, not answering her question. "Don't worry, babe, I'll still respect you in the morning," he murmured, brushing his hand lightly over her hair. "It's been pretty rough the past few weeks and we both need our rest. I'll see you tomorrow."

"I think it's time that you humor me." Jaime's voice was a seductive purr.

Mac's smile faded at the silvery mist in her eyes. His own eyes had darkened to a purple hue as they focused on the enticing shape of her lips.

"We haven't finished celebrating yet," she admonished huskily, moving forward at a leisurely pace. Her hands flattened against his chest, sending prickles of heat through the soft fabric of his shirt. When Mac opened his mouth to speak, one hand lifted so that her fingers could press against his lips. "No words, darling." Her hands now slid along his shoulders and down his arms.

Mac couldn't find the strength to resist when Jaime led him into the bedroom. She positioned him next to the bed, then stepped away to pull back the quilt and top sheet.

When he began to undo his shirt, she brushed his hands away. "Let me," she purred, taking her time in releasing the buttons. With each one she undid, she treated the flesh revealed to a moist kiss. After pushing the shirt off his shoulders and dropping it to the carpet, she began working on his slacks. She unbuckled the belt deftly, but before she lowered the zipper, her palm pressed daringly against him. Mac's swift indrawn breath only echoed the pulsing against her hand.

"Jaime," he groaned softly.

"Soon," she promised with the air of a determined seductress. She lowered the zipper and her hands circled the waistband of his briefs. Then Jaime bent down and pressed a kiss against the taut skin of his stomach. "You have a very sexy body, Mac," she murmured.

She was jerked upward and hauled against him. Mac's mouth fastened hungrily on hers, his tongue plunging into her mouth.

Jaime pulled away and swept out of his reach. "This is my treat," she informed him, standing close enough to push him onto the bed. Her idea of seducing him had purely been on impulse, but now that she had started, she certainly wasn't going to stop. She was thankful that she had decided to go back to taking precautions after their first night together. She might have been safe that time, but she couldn't take risks like that again. Not when their passions could erupt so suddenly and without warning. She wanted nothing to mar this evening. "And my rules."

Mac looked up and watched with glazed eyes as Jaime leisurely unbuttoned her blouse and dropped it to the carpet, leaving her shoulders bare except for the lacy straps of her creamy silk camisole. She took her time undoing the buttons along the side of her pants. Her fingertips circled the waistband of her pantyhose before pulling them off. Seeing her now clad only in the camisole and a pair of minuscule bikini briefs, Mac could feel the force building up in his body until he felt ready to explode. Every pulsating vein screamed to reach up and pull her down to him and take what she was blatantly offering, but he was going to play by her rules. Even if it killed him!

"Did I ever tell you what a sexy body you have, Mac?" Jaime asked in a soft conversational tone. "Oh, you're much more than a pair of broad shoulders, trim waist, and tight backside. Did you know that there's a nerve near your shoulder that jumps when I kiss you there? There's also a very interesting indentation along your spine that dips when—"

"*Jaime!*" Mac pleaded, watching her fingertips tease the lace waistband of her bikini pants. "I'm not going to be able to take much more if you want me all in one piece."

She leaned over, a bent knee on the bed for balance as she brushed her lips across his. "You deserve a very special night, Mac," she breathed, retreating just long enough to dispose of her camisole and bikini pants before returning to the bed and an eager Mac.

Jaime settled her hands on Mac's shoulders and nipped lightly at the sensitive skin of his throat.

Mac could feel the pressure building until his ears rang. He couldn't remember a woman ever seducing him the way Jaime was now. His hips arched up when her leg slid between his and rubbed along his muscular calves and thighs. So this was what she felt when he made love to her! This racing of the blood, the shafts of fire piercing the flesh, and the lack of air in the lungs.

"I always did like salty men." Jaime laughed throatily before fastening her teeth on a tiny male nipple.

"You're driving me insane!" he gasped, digging his fingers into her hair. He had to touch her! Her inquisitive hand sliding along the taut surface of his abdomen and her own nipples brushing against his chest were making him lose what little control he had left.

"Just relax and enjoy." Her tongue traced a circle around each nipple, then drew an imaginary line down to his navel.

"Who can relax?" Mac gritted, knowing that a strange lack of air was responsible for the red mist before his eyes. He gulped, taking deep breaths when Jaime reached her goal. Unintelligible words dropped from his lips as his fingers dug further into her hair. Her lips and tongue were a burning sweetness to his pleasurable agony. When Jaime slid back up his body and captured him with her warmth, he was past the point of sanity. Their bodies gleamed with sweat as she took him into the sensual fantasy world they had shared before.

Afterward Mac lay on his back with a drowsy Jaime curled up against his side.

"My God." He uttered a brief laugh. His hands trembled as they soothed along her arms and her breasts. "So that's what it's like to be seduced."

"Did I please you?" There was a hint of shyness in her voice. There had been no doubt in Mac's mind that Jaime hadn't acted this way with another man and the thought pleased him.

"Please me?" Mac hugged her tightly. "Baby, no one has ever given me what you just did. I may not recover for a long while."

Jaime murmured indistinctly as she allowed sleep to overtake her. Mac merely smiled and cuddled her closer to him as he also drifted off to sleep. It was a night that wouldn't be easily forgotten.

"I'd like to ask a favor of you," Mac mentioned during lunch a week later at what had become their favorite seafood restaurant. "I was wondering if you would help organize a party to celebrate our getting the Royalton bid."

"Organize?" She looked at him curiously, her calm gray gaze

131

doing funny things to his equilibrium. "You mean plan a menu and drinks and such?"

"That's about it." He grinned sheepishly. "My idea of a party is five guys over for poker, serving them beer and potato chips. Everyone in the office worked a lot of hours to help pull this off and I'd like to do something special for them. I also thought about inviting a few of the other contractors we'll be working with on this."

"Where do you want to hold it?" Jaime dipped her calamari into the sauce then popped it into her mouth.

"My house. I thought the Saturday after next would be good. Would you be willing to help out?" Mac watched her with hopeful eyes, adding, "Just as long as you don't serve squid!"

"Calamari," she corrected, dipping another piece into the sauce. "And it's not some exotic food like rattlesnake meat."

He grimaced while watching her eat. "I'd rather have the rattlesnake meat."

"I'll do it," she replied, adding sincerely, "I promise to do you proud."

"You already have." His voice was heavy with meaning, sending a faint flush to her cheeks. "I enjoy making you blush," he teased.

"A redhead's curse." She sighed dramatically. "You better tell me how many people you plan to invite and I'll figure out the hors d'oeuvres from there. You better be prepared to do some work on this too because I don't intend to do everything and let you get all the credit!"

Mac reached into the pocket of his jeans, drew out a shiny piece of metal, and tossed it onto the table in front of her.

"In case you want to get into my house when I'm not there," he explained in an all too casual voice.

Jaime looked down at the key lying on the table. The idea of having such easy access to his house gave her a strange feeling in the pit of her stomach.

132

"Aren't you afraid I'll go in and rearrange your furniture?" she teased huskily, looking up at him.

"Honey, if you want to rearrange the whole house, feel free." He smiled warmly.

"Hm, a temptation I can't refuse." She picked up the key and dropped it into her purse. "We better get going. You promised Ray you'd be out at the site by two o'clock and you're going to be late as it is."

"Not much longer before spring will be here," he commented, as they walked outside toward his truck.

Even with her wool coat on, Jaime shivered in the cold winter air and looked up at him with disbelief. "I hope you don't mind if I'm in a hurry for spring to arrive," she said dryly.

He grinned as he turned on the ignition and switched on the heater full blast to quickly warm the truck's cold interior. "I never saw anyone with an aversion to cold like you." He looked down as she snuggled up next to him. "Although there're times when I enjoy that particular dislike." He tipped her face up for a brief kiss on the lips.

"Let's just say that I'm happiest when the sun is out and I can leave my coat at home." Her lips tingled at his possession and her tongue briefly skimmed over her moist mouth to recall the taste of his kiss.

During this time, Jaime worked closely with the clerks while they took turns going to school to learn the new computer system. Since the same system had been used in her previous job, Jaime didn't need to worry about taking the time off to attend the classes.

Having felt guilty of neglecting her mother during this busy period, Jaime arranged to meet her for dinner.

"You seem to be enjoying your work a great deal," Eileen commented when they met at a nearby restaurant the next evening.

"There's enough variety there," Jaime replied. She picked at

133

her crepe filled with shrimp and mushrooms and covered with a creamy wine sauce.

Eileen ate heartily of her crab salad. "I picked up some brochures on cruises in the Greek isles," she commented. "I thought it might be a nice change for me. Madilyn Norris, you remember her? Janice's mother? She's been interested in going on a cruise also and we thought we might go together."

Jaime looked up with a bright smile. That was just what her mother needed; to get out and meet new people. Madilyn Norris was full of energy and a notorious busybody. She was a perfect complement to the shy, quiet Eileen.

"I think it would do you a world of good," Jaime approved wholeheartedly, lifting her glass of wine in a toast. "You'll have to be sure and send me plenty of postcards so I know you're getting out and seeing the sights."

Eileen smiled, looking brighter than she had in months. "Of course, I'll have to buy a new wardrobe," she mused.

"Um, my favorite occupation, spending other people's money." Jaime laughed. "Let's go out first thing Saturday and see what we can find."

"That would be just perfect," the older woman told her. "We could go out for brunch too."

The balance of their meal spent making plans for their shopping spree.

When Jaime finally got home that evening, she went into her bedroom and quickly stripped off her clothes, then put on a nightgown and robe before going into the bathroom to cream off her makeup and wash her face.

While she was lying in bed, her thoughts wandered back to the two times she and Mac had made love. There had been no repeats of either night and Mac never spoke of them, although there were times she could feel the tension building up in his body as he kissed her. Why was he holding back all of a sudden? It wasn't any lack of desire on his part and certainly not on hers! She would have thought those nights had been a figment of her imagination if it hadn't been for the potent memories of Mac's hard body claiming hers.

There was no longer any way to dampen the flame of Jaime's desire. The strong passions underlying her personality could no longer be denied. Jaime shifted restlessly. Even the memories were enough to stir her. She rolled over on her stomach and pulled her pillow over her head, ordering her body to settle down. Yet with all the turmoil running through her mind, it was a long time before she fell into a deep sleep.

The following Monday morning, Jaime was surprised to find a note from Mac on her desk. She was glad she was alone as her eager fingers ripped the envelope open. Her face betrayed her disappointment as she quickly scanned the contents. He wanted to let her know how many people would be invited to the party and not to worry about invitations. Sue was taking care of those. He ended the note by saying how confident he was that Jaime could handle the party preparations with her usual ease.

"I should go out and buy pretzels and potato chips," she murmured as she crumpled the note and tossed it into the wastebasket.

Jaime was glad that Mac wasn't in his office that day or she would have gone up to tell him what he could do with his party. Instead she sat down at her desk and jotted down a few ideas for hors d'oeuvres that wouldn't require a lot of time to make.

She had arranged to arrive at Mac's house in the afternoon the day of the party so she would have plenty of time to set things up.

"You're welcome to change at my place," Mac had offered with a wicked twinkle in his eyes. Jaime had accepted his offer with a charm-filled smile.

Dressed in worn jeans and a dark-green wool sweater and carrying a small makeup case and her outfit on a hanger, she followed Mac's instructions to his house in Dana Point.

Jaime wasn't sure what she had expected, but a gray Cape Cod with white shutters and a widow's walk wasn't it.

The front door opened and Mac walked out, looking very virile. He was wearing faded nylon athletic shorts and a football jersey cut off at the midriff.

"You look surprised," he greeted her. "What did you expect, an old beach shack?" There was a hint of the old bitterness in his voice.

Jaime was taken aback by his sudden personality switch. "If it's as lovely inside as it is out, you're a lucky man," she told him.

His eyes searched her face but could only read sincerity in the delicate features. "There's still a lot of work to do," he replied gruffly, turning to lead the way inside. "I'm a builder, not an interior decorator."

The pieces of furniture in the living room were few, but of good quality. Jaime absently ran a hand over the cushioned back of a salmon-color tweed couch. Her eyes were then drawn to one wall housing a built-in aquarium.

"Your one concession to modernity?" She flashed him a sly glance.

"They're relaxing." He shrugged. "Undemanding company in the evenings."

Jaime glanced curiously at Mac, who had again adopted the tense stance he had shown before. The accused man awaiting the jury's verdict. She walked over to the floor-to-ceiling multipaned window and looked out at the ocean. To her right was an old-fashioned rolltop desk turned so that the person sitting there could enjoy the view. The oyster-colored drapes were drawn back and looked as if they were rarely closed, but then why should they shut out such a magnificent sight?

Jaime turned to face Mac. "It's beautiful," she said enthusiastically.

His body visibly relaxed. "You better see the rest before you make your decision," he said gruffly.

The kitchen also boasted many windows with a view of the

136

bluffs across the highway. The colonial theme wasn't ruined by the addition of modern appliances, thanks to clever arranging.

"I have the food in the car." Jaime glanced around the kitchen, instantly liking its light and airy feeling.

"I'll help you carry it in," he offered.

After they brought the necessary supplies inside, Mac told Jaime he was just about to go running.

"Keeps the kinks out of the old body," he explained with a grin.

Jaime shot him a wry glance, her eyes moving over the lean body and well-muscled legs. For the owner of an old body, Mac looked very well preserved.

"I'll help you when I get back in an hour or so." He walked toward the front door. "My housekeeper came by yesterday, so everything should be in order. Feel free to use anything you might need. Dishes are in the cabinet to the right of the sink."

Oddly, Jaime didn't feel as strange working in Mac's house as she thought she might. In no time she had various salted nuts in dishes on tables and perishable snacks stored in the refrigerator. A quick glance in the main bathroom told her that guest towels had already been laid out.

She was tempted to go upstairs to see the bedrooms but quickly squelched the thought. If she did go up there, what did she think she'd find? An article of woman's clothing? Blond hairs on the pillow?

The thought of another woman being in Mac's bedroom was suddenly more than Jaime could bear. She turned and walked quickly back into the living room, where she sat brooding, silently watching the quiet antics of the tropical fish.

"They're better than any tranquilizer." Mac's quiet voice startled her.

"You're back." Her observation was unnecessary.

"I didn't think you wanted me to greet my guests dressed like this." He cocked an amused eyebrow. His dark hair was damp, plastered to his head. His sweat-stained shirt clung to his chest while his shorts had molded themselves to his body, leaving nothing to the imagination. Jaime watched him, fascinated.

"I believe you said I could use your guest room to change in," she murmured.

"Or the master bedroom if you'd prefer." He grinned wickedly.

"The guest room will be just fine." Jaime smiled back.

"Upstairs and to the left," Mac told her as he walked into the kitchen. "I guess I can't mess things up too much by getting a can of beer."

Jaime never believed in spending hours getting herself ready for a party. Her routine was very much the same as her daily one, except she used a stronger, headier perfume, a heavier hand with her makeup, and she took more time with her hair. As always, the end result was perfection.

Her hair had been artfully arranged to frame her face and her makeup had a golden sheen to it. A narrow bronze silk skirt skimmed past her hips and dropped to the floor in graceful folds. She wore a matching camisole top, edged with a deeper color lace along the curved neckline; a bronze-and-black striped kimono-style jacket completed the provocative outfit. Glancing at the clock, she hurried with her final preparations. She wanted to be downstairs before anyone arrived.

When she entered the living room, she was due for another surprise. Mac had showered and changed and was there ahead of her. Gone were the old clothes; now he wore navy slacks and a light-gray shirt open at the throat. His hair still gleamed damply from his shower, its luxuriant thickness barely tamed. His expression was openly appreciative when he greeted Jaime.

"It's a shame all those people are due here in the next half hour." There was a husky note in his voice. "There're going to be some men here who won't be able to keep their hands off you, especially me."

Jaime blinked, surprised by the harsh note in his voice. "I'm

138

sure I can handle anything, or anyone, that may come my way," she replied calmly.

She wasn't given the chance to find out, since Mac stuck close to her side once the people began arriving. First Sue and Ray came with Gina and her fiancé behind them.

Mac was a gracious host, making sure to greet each newcomer and ensuring they met the other guests. Everyone was made to feel at home.

"You deserve a lot of credit for making this party a success," Sue told Jaime. "These shrimp rolls are delicious." She paused and nodded toward a basket of cut flowers set on a low table behind the couch. "You've also added a much-needed woman's touch to this barn, even if it's only temporary."

"I like this house," Jaime protested. "Mac has a fantastic view of the ocean from here."

"Hm, I heard the view from the bedroom is much better," Sue commented slyly, without malice.

"Oh? Who did you hear that from?" Jaime had a sinking feeling in her stomach. Had Mac made love to another woman in the past few weeks?

"She heard it from me." An arm encircled Jaime's waist and pulled her back against a warm body. "Would you care to confirm the rumor?" he murmured, nuzzling the soft skin just behind her ear and sending tremors through her body.

"No, thank you," she said pertly, picking up a shrimp roll and slipping it between Mac's lips. "They say food is an excellent substitute for sex. Perhaps you should try it sometime," she advised dryly.

"Maybe that's why I never have a weight problem." He moved away before Jaime could give in to her temptation to hit him.

"Ah, to be young and lusty again." Sue sighed, ignoring Jaime's glare.

"Not when only one side is doing the lusting," Jaime muttered under her breath, walking toward the kitchen to refill a tray with more cheese puffs.

"Great party, Jaime!" A man's slurring voice sounded close to her ear.

She turned around, recoiling at florid features pressed too close to her own. "Mr. MacMasters is the one to take the credit, Mr. Laughlin," she replied, keeping her voice smooth as cream, trying to avoid a scene with Mac's business associates. "If you'll excuse me, I have to return to the guests."

"Mac always said you had a lot of class, and I can sure see it for myself tonight," he told her, snaking a probing hand around her waist and moving upward to the curve of her breast. "What do you say to going somewhere after this thing is over? Somewhere where the two of us can be alone?" He leered suggestively. "Someone as good-looking and sexy as you should have a man around."

Jaime jerked away and faced him with a glacial stare. "As far as I'm concerned, the last thing I need in my life is a man, *any* man. Get the idea?"

"If he doesn't, I'll give him a more explicit picture." Mac's cold drawl fell on their ears. Mr. Laughlin's face paled and he turned away, muttering an excuse.

"I saw Laughlin making too many trips to the bar and decided I better keep an eye on him," Mac said as he walked into the kitchen.

"I had him under control," Jaime argued, her temper now directed at Mac.

His features darkened. "You could have fooled me. The man's business ethics are impeccable, but his private life is a little too wild, and I wouldn't have liked it if I had found his hands on you." His eyes glowed darkly.

Jaime knew her temper was now on the verge of boiling over. "I shouldn't think you, of all people, would mind!" she snapped, thrusting a tray in his hands and brushing past him. "Here, you're the host, *you* serve the cheese puffs!"

When she returned to the living room, only the spark in her eyes betrayed her anger, but the smile on her lips could melt the coldest heart. She was bright and vivacious, a charming addition to any party, although she kept well out of Mr. Laughlin's reach.

She also kept her senses alert to Mac's presence. Each time he approached a group she was with, she graciously took her leave to speak to someone else. The gleam in his eyes told her he knew her intent and promised his own form of revenge . . . later. She was determined not to be present for it.

Jaime was exhausted by the time the guests began to leave. Sue and Ray were among the last to go, and before they did, Sue took her aside for a quickly whispered piece of advice. It hadn't taken the older woman long to notice the battle of wills going on between Jaime and Mac.

"Since it looks like the real fight of the century will be going on soon, all I can say is fake him out. Let Mac believe that nothing is wrong as far as you're concerned. That way you'll throw his strategy completely off." Sue smiled and gave Jaime's arm a reassuring squeeze. "See you Monday," she said encouragingly as she approached her husband, who had been standing near the front door talking to Mac.

CHAPTER NINE

While Mac walked outside with Sue and Ray, Jaime moved around the living room picking up empty dishes and filled ashtrays and carrying them into the kitchen.

"You don't have to do that," Mac protested, as he walked back inside. "I can clean up in the morning."

"No one in their right mind would leave this mess overnight." She shook her head with disapproval. She moved over to open a few windows to air out the smoke-filled room, pausing to take in a breath of cold, salty air.

Mac walked up behind her and slid his arms around her waist in an attempt to pull her back against him. He nibbled lazily along the side of her neck with teasing bites. "You made the party a success," he murmured.

"I—ah—I have to do the dishes." She issued a faint protest, discovering she was having difficulty in breathing.

"Leave them." One hand tunneled under her top to find her bare breast. "Um, I was right, I didn't think you were wearing a bra," he said huskily. "Don't go, Jaime, stay here . . . with me."

She closed her eyes, tipping her head to one side to allow Mac easier access to the sensitive areas of her neck and ear. "It's late." Her argument sounded weak to her ears when all she wanted to do was rediscover the delights of that first night with Mac so long ago, but she'd be damned if she'd allow him to think she'd tumble into his bed at the snap of his fingers!

"All the more reason for you to stay. It's dangerous for a

woman to be on the road alone at this hour of the night," he murmured, seducing her with the husky tones of his voice as he teased. "After all, it isn't as if you have a dog or cat to feed or plants to water or even an angry husband waiting up for you."

Jaime rested her head back against the curve of his shoulder, reveling in the animal warmth he exuded. She knew instinctively that any argument she presented would be effectively shot down, and at this point she didn't think she would have the power to move away from his embrace.

"I'll even serve you breakfast in bed." Mac's voice grew thicker with desire.

"I rarely eat breakfast," she breathed sharply as his thumb and forefinger teased her nipple into an aching hardness.

"Okay, I'll serve you lunch then. Anything to please the lady."

She tried to turn around and seek the heat of Mac's mouth, but his hold merely tightened to prevent her from moving. "Mac." Her gasping plea was lost as he abruptly spun her around and hungrily possessed her mouth with an urgency equaled only by her own.

Jaime was molded tightly against Mac's hardening body. His hands slid down her spine to cup her buttocks and lift her up, pulling her against his masculinity. He wanted her so badly that the ache in his lower body was instantly transmitted to her. Her hands swept over his nape and fluttered down to his shoulders. Her body moved sensuously against his.

"Oh, no." Mac drew ragged breaths to give his body some semblance of control. He pushed a disheveled Jaime slightly away from him. "We're having the comfort of my bed for our night together. I'm too old for these acrobatics."

She managed a shaky laugh, which halted when she saw the purple flames in Mac's eyes threatening to consume her at any moment.

"Poor baby," she mocked lovingly, running her palm along his cheekbone down to his jaw. He gripped her arm and turned it so he could press his lips against the sensitive skin of her wrist, teasing the center of her palm with the tip of his tongue. His mouth moved up to consume each finger and graze the tips with his teeth, stopping to heal them with the moist heat of his lips. Jaime's eyes were captured by Mac's intense gaze. "Mac," she breathed, unable to say any more than his name, but that was all that was needed.

Mac wrapped an arm around her shoulders and led her across the living room, turning the lights off along the way. They climbed the stairs slowly in silence, needing no words to convey the emotions they felt. There was no need to hurry now. They both knew what they wanted, and the outcome was inevitable.

When they entered Mac's darkened bedroom, he switched on a small bedside lamp. Then, turning back to her, he uttered, "No." His rasping voice halted her as she reached around searching for the zipper to her top. "I want the luxury of undressing you."

His fingers were cool against her heated skin as he slid the zipper down and carefully slipped the camisole over her head. He knelt to remove her silk skirt, pantyhose, and lacy bikini briefs. When he finished, he leaned forward and kissèd her navel. Jaime couldn't hold back a moan when his tongue dipped into the tiny indentation. She gripped his shoulders, afraid that her legs wouldn't hold her.

Mac stood up slowly, pausing to drop moist, heated kisses along the way; on her midriff, the tips of each breast, and the hollow where her pulse pounded erratically. For a moment he stood up and looked at her naked form.

"Now it's your turn," he invited quietly.

Jaime's fingers trembled as she unbuttoned and pulled Mac's shirt off. As the masculine beauty of his chest was revealed, she couldn't help but stop for a moment to kiss each nipple in the same manner he had done to her. The rigid tension in his body told her the strain she was placing on him. Her fingers felt a little more sure as they unfastened his belt and reached for the zipper of his slacks. When his briefs and slacks fell to the carpet, he

144

stepped out of the pile of clothing and faced her squarely. Jaime watched Mac quietly, savoring the pleasure of looking at him.

Mac walked over to the bed and threw back the covers before turning back to Jaime. She stood in the middle of the room, not sure if it was the cold or the force of her desire that caused her to tremble so. She took his outstretched hand and walked over to the bed, allowing him to press her back gently onto the sheets. When Mac stretched out beside her, she turned her head questioningly toward the small lamp then back at him.

"No." He correctly interpreted her question. "I want to see you this time. I'm selfish, Jaime. I not only want to hear your cries of love, I want to see the expression on your face when I take you over the edge with me," he growled, nuzzling her throat.

"Just one second," Jaime whispered, pressing her palm against his chest when he moved to lower his body against hers. For just one more moment, she wanted to enjoy the power she had over him. "It seems you're pretty sure of yourself if you think you can just tumble me into your bed and have your way with me. I have half a mind to get up from here, get dressed, and leave," she threatened, although the expression in her eyes told him how faint her threat was.

Mac's husky laugh sent shivers along her spine, while his teeth fastened on her earlobe transmitted a different kind of shiver throughout her body. "It's been pure hell not touching you like this." His hands slid down her side to grasp her arching hips. "I've had my reasons."

"I'd be interested to hear them." She fought a losing battle against the shafts of fire in her veins at his intimate touch.

Mac buried his face in her fragrant, silky hair. "You mean more to me than you'll ever know, Jaime," he mumbled. "I didn't want you to think I only wanted you in my bed. You're far more than that to me. Oh, I know I'm doing it backward, but I was trying to show you that I respected you by keeping my

145

distance," he finished humbly. "Let me tell you, it wasn't easy either."

"John MacMasters, I could strangle you for playing the tease!" Jaime pushed her fist into his rock-hard stomach. This was far from what she had expected to hear.

"Tease, you want to talk about tease?" he growled, raising his head to look down at her. "What about the way your delectable bottom wiggles when you walk or the way your tongue slides out over your lower lip when you're concentrating on something, not to mention when you don't wear a bra under some of those heavy sweaters. Those sexy little camisoles you women seem to prefer nowadays sure don't help my libido any! *You're* the one who's the tease, Clarke."

"Oh?" Jaime kept her voice low and provocative. "Like this?" The tip of her tongue darted out to glide over her lip.

Mac's groan was deep in his throat as he captured her mouth, his teeth pulling gently on her sensual lower lip. "A tease," he groaned, "a seductress guaranteed to steal a man's sanity." His fingers slid through the coppery silk of her hair and brought it to his lips. Feather-light kisses, all the more intoxicating for their restrained passion, rained over her face beginning at her forehead and moving down to caress her delicately arched brows, her closed eyelids, her nose. His lips finally came to rest in the faint hollow above her upper lip.

Jaime's tongue snaked out to taste the salty-rough texture of Mac's chin. She drew her head back so that she could look up at his face taut with emotion. "No more talk, Mac," she whispered, letting her hands gliding along the muscular hollows of his body tell him the rest. "There're other ways to tell me how you feel."

For a brief moment his eyes were brooding as he studied her face shrouded in the shadows. "I only wish I was good enough for you, Jaime." Even as he spoke, he couldn't stop his hands from moving down to knead her bare hips and trace the moist skin, evoking a shudder of longing from her.

146

She reached up swiftly to press her fingertips against his lips. "MacMasters, you talk too much." Her other hand ran along his body and tantalized his velvety-hard skin.

Jaime's intimate caress broke the last of Mac's barriers. Soon she was writhing beneath his sensual touch, oblivious to all but the intense pleasure he was giving her.

Mac's throaty growl echoed in the caverns of Jaime's mouth even as his body captured hers. There was no coyness or holding back on either side; only the desire to give the other pleasure.

Mac wasn't content to just find his release with Jaime. He wanted her to climb each mountain beside him, to die that small death with him. He was her seducer, her lover, her partner; he was all she needed to survive. Her hands roamed possessively over the moist skin of his back and gripped his hips, afraid he would leave her to her fate. Mac unerringly found each sensitized nerve on her body. When Jaime's cry eventually broke past her lips, it was smothered by the rough covering of Mac's mouth growling that same cry of satisfaction.

It was a long while before either could find the breath to speak. Mac had rolled away, but he made sure to keep Jaime close against his side. He pressed her cheek against the hardened pillow of his chest. When he felt a faint dampness on her face, he looked down at her with concern.

"Did I hurt you, love?" he murmured. "I'm sorry if I got a little rough. I just go crazy when you touch me and I can't stop myself."

She smiled and shook her head. "I think these are another kind of tears." She lay quietly with her eyes closed, feeling replete and pleasantly drowsy.

Mac lowered his head and licked each tear from her cheeks. No woman had ever given him as much of herself as Jaime had that night. The extent of her passion had surprised and delighted him, and he knew that even greater pleasure awaited them in the future.

"You're not falling asleep on me, are you?" His deep voice rumbled in his chest.

"Um." Jaime gave a sleepy nod, still keeping her eyes closed. Her arm lay across his chest as she snuggled even closer. "I'm only recharging my batteries. Something tells me this won't be the only time tonight," she said with a chuckle.

Mac's laughter was rich and full-bodied like a fine wine. "Very much the lady in public, very much the wanton in the bedroom. What am I going to do with you?"

Jaime's hand strayed over his chest and down to his flat stomach and lower. "Oh, I'm sure you'll think of something," she purred, listening to his harsh indrawn breath at her intimate touch.

"You're insatiable," he accused in a thick voice, reaching down to grasp her teasing fingers and halt their exploration.

"I thought I was supposed to say that about you," she countered.

Mac rolled over and imprisoned Jaime under his body. His hands cupped her face, his thumbs probing gently the corners of her mouth.

"Why you?" he mused in his husky voice. "How can a skinny woman like you turn me on just with that sexy walk of yours? All you have to do is look at me with those big gray eyes and I feel like a stallion let loose among a herd of mares, except there's only one mare who could satisfy me. You talk to me in that oh-so-very prim and proper voice and all I want to do is destroy that virginal facade and reveal the wanton hussy underneath."

"You already did." Her lips twitched.

"Only for me," he whispered urgently, then he repeated with what almost sounded like a cry of desperation, "Why you?"

Sobered by this sudden, intense side of the man, Jaime stroked his cheek lightly with her fingertips. Was he regretting what had just happened between them? Was he wishing for a woman with more experience? All she knew was that she wanted to give him the pleasure he had given her and the only way she could do that was to follow her instincts, but would that be enough for him?

"You excite me like nobody else, Clarke." His husky whisper was warm against her shoulder as his lips searched her bare skin. "When I have you in my arms, I feel as if nothing can go wrong."

He didn't regret it after all! her heart sang out. Jaime's arms tightened. "I want you again, Mac," she told him, now not afraid to voice her desires out loud.

Grinning crookedly, he lifted his head to look at her. "Whatever the lady wishes."

This time their sensual exploration was more leisurely. While there was no explosive coming together, there was something warmer and richer in their lovemaking. Jaime again experienced that airless climb, with Mac patiently leading every step of the way striding beside her in that ultimate sharing. Later, when she finally fell asleep, Jaime was very much aware of his arms holding her as if afraid to release her, but that was all right. The last thing she wanted was to be apart from this man. They both slept deeply, but even in sleep they didn't loosen their hold on each other.

Jaime awoke slowly the next morning. With her eyes still closed, she languorously reached out to touch Mac's body but she encountered only cool sheets. Immediately wide awake, Jaime sat up and looked around the bedroom. It suddenly felt empty and she felt very alone. She hitched the blankets up around her bare shoulders against the chilly air and wondered where he had gone.

Perhaps this room best reflected Mac's personality, she thought. While the furniture was made of a dark wood she didn't recognize, it wasn't imposing. It filled the large room, yet didn't crowd it.

A framed colored lithograph hung over the chest of drawers. Heavy cream-colored drapes flowed down to a rich lapis-blue carpet that matched the narrow stripes in the comforter on the

149

bed. A creamy beige easy chair sat in one corner next to a tall bookcase overflowing with many volumes. Jaime leaned forward, curious about the titles of the books but reluctant to leave her warm nest.

"Good morning, sleepyhead."

She turned her head, smiling brightly at her visitor. Mac wore only a pair of faded jeans, giving her a sight of the bare chest she had so happily mapped out with her fingers and lips the night before. "You're up early," she commented.

Mac shook his head and laughed. He walked over to the bed and leaned down to kiss Jaime on the lips. "I've been up for about a half an hour," he replied. "As it's past noon, neither one of us is up too early. I came up to see if you were awake yet so I could finish cooking breakfast."

Jaime linked her arms around his neck. She looked innocent and sensual at the same time. She was the picture of a woman content with herself. "Um, I adore a man who serves me breakfast in bed," she breathed, pressing small kisses to his throat.

Mac's body tensed at her words. "Have you had many men serve you breakfast in bed?"

Startled by his dark voice, Jaime drew back. "And how many women have slept here ahead of me?" she accused, dreading to think of the number he would probably give her.

"None. You're the first." He spoke quietly, leaving her in no doubt as to the truth of his words.

"It must be a very new bed, then," she snapped, pulling her arms back.

Mac pulled her back into his arms and buried his face against her neck. "Let's not fight, Jaime," he murmured. "Sometimes I feel we'll have little time together as it is and it shouldn't be spent arguing. Until you, I've never brought any woman up here. You have to believe me." His eyes pleaded with her.

"You're beginning to sound like a prophet of doom," she muttered. "Can't you ever have any happy thoughts?"

"Only when I'm holding you in my arms." His hand brushed

a stray curl from her face. "I think that's where I should keep you all the time."

"I could settle for that," she murmured, nuzzling his throat with her lips.

Just as his mouth was about to cover hers, they both heard a low rumbling sound. It was her stomach.

"Okay, I get the hint." Mac chuckled as he pulled away. "You've got fifteen minutes to get downstairs for breakfast."

"What? Don't I get served breakfast in bed?" She affected a little girl's pout. "You promised."

"No way. If I brought it up here, I have a feeling it would never be eaten." He straightened up. "There're extra towels in the bathroom if you want to take a shower before breakfast."

Jaime showered and washed her hair in record time, not wanting to be apart from Mac for any longer than necessary. After wrapping her wet hair in a towel, she took a short terrycloth robe from the hook on the back of the door and slipped it on. Belting it tightly around her waist, she walked downstairs, her appetite whetted by the fragrant odors that filled the air.

"What smells so good?" Jaime called out, as she entered the kitchen.

"Scrambled eggs and sausage." Mac handed her a cup filled with steaming coffee. His half-closed eyes roamed over Jaime as she stood there enveloped in the oversized robe. His mind recalled the feel and texture of the satiny skin hidden by the thick material. "Until now I never knew anyone could look sexy in something like that." His husky voice indicated that his mind was no longer on breakfast.

A faint pink covered Jaime's cheeks. She walked over to the stove and deftly turned the eggs onto two plates and added the sausage links.

"Here, I think you're growing weak from hunger." She set the plates on the small table in the corner. "You're also in need of glasses because I'm not your everyday glamorous type in the morning when my hair is wrapped up in a towel and I don't have any makeup on." She seated herself at a small oval table in one corner of the room.

Mac's thumb and forefinger reached down to capture her chin and tilt it upward. "Personally, I think you've never been sexier than in that robe without a stitch on underneath and your face scrubbed clean. In fact, I think I like the real you even more," he whispered, just before his mouth rubbed sensually over hers.

"Mac," Jaime murmured moments later, when their lips finally parted. "Your food is getting cold."

He growled something uncomplimentary about the food before recapturing her lips again. He pulled her out of the chair and into his arms, stopping only when the low rumble in Jaime's stomach sounded again. Laughing sardonically, Mac released her and announced they better eat fast.

"I don't want us to miss out on the rest of the day," Mac murmured when they had finished eating. "What would you say to driving down the coast and having dinner with me?"

"I'd have to go home and change my clothes first." She was pleased that he hadn't intended to send her home after breakfast with a vague "see you tomorrow."

"I'll follow you home and we can leave from there. Now why don't you go upstairs and get dressed while I finish cleaning up the mess I've made," he suggested.

It didn't take Jaime long to finish towel drying her hair and to brush it into some semblance of order before dressing in the jeans and green sweater she had worn when she arrived the day before. Then Mac went upstairs to change. He came down looking even more virile than before, wearing a pale-yellow long-sleeved shirt and a navy V-necked sweater draped casually over his shoulders with the sleeves looped over his chest.

During the drive to her house, Jaime was all too aware of the dark car following her. She parked her Porsche in the carport and led the way inside the house, murmuring to Mac that it wouldn't take her long to change.

With a speed that astonished even her, Jaime changed into a

pair of dark-green cords and a matching striped shirt. When she walked into the living room, Mac glanced up from a magazine.

"I was getting myself prepared for a long wait," he told her, as he held up the magazine. "By now I should know better."

Jaime halted in the middle of the room, her entire being stunned by the force of Mac's easy grin. Suddenly the realization hit her like a ton of bricks. She was in love with him! As surely as the sun rose in the east every morning, she, Jaime Lynn Clarke, had fallen in love with John MacMasters! She, who had always dreamed of a suave and debonair prince, had fallen in love with a man so down to earth and tender that it was frightening.

Alarmed by her pale face, Mac dropped his magazine and jumped to his feet.

"Jaime, are you all right?" he demanded, frowning with concern.

Fearing he might read this new knowledge in her eyes, she hastily lowered her lashes and replied softly, "I'm fine. Shall we go?" She walked over to the closet and took out a tan suede jacket.

During their drive down the coast, Mac stole concerned glances at Jaime from time to time. He was clearly puzzled by her suddenly quiet demeanor, which was so unlike her.

The realization that she loved Mac had shocked Jaime, yet it would explain why she had fallen so easily into his bed last night. She certainly hadn't tried to resist him very much. There could only be one reason why.

Turning away to look out the window, Jaime felt overpowered by the raw emotions coursing through her body.

"Bored with me already?" Mac's low voice filled her ears.

Never, she thought. You couldn't bore me in a hundred years, even if I didn't talk to another human being in that time. But she didn't reveal her thoughts. "I guess I'm a little tired," she murmured.

"Hm, I wonder why." Mac's lazy smile held a hint of male

satisfaction. Without taking his eyes from the road, he reached out and caressed the nape of her neck with his fingertips.

"You're not very humble, are you?" Jaime's voice trembled under the sensual touch.

"I would be if I thought it would help."

Jaime closed her eyes against the intensity of Mac's voice. All her senses were alert. She was afraid of his finding out her love for him. Oh, how he'd gloat to find out that she could fall as hard as his little blondes!

Mac drove until they reached Del Mar. What had once been a sleepy little beach community outside San Diego had grown up with the introduction of beach homes of all sizes and descriptions.

He parked the car near a popular seafood restaurant that faced the ocean. As Jaime got out of the car, she looked around and thought of the first place Mac had taken her to. It seemed so long ago!

"Not like my chili dog joint, is it?" Mac had read her mind again.

"I wish you would stop walking in and out of my mind," she said, exasperation showing in her voice.

"Why?" His soft voice turned husky as his hand rose to stroke her neck. "I'd let you walk in and out of my mind anytime. No invitation needed."

Turning her head, Jaime felt a tingling throughout her entire being from the strong fingers ruffling the ends of her hair. Mac's forehead creased in a puzzled frown as he gazed down at her face. He couldn't understand the expression in her smoky gray eyes. What question was she silently asking him? He felt its importance, yet the question eluded him. For once he couldn't find entrance to the innermost regions of her mind.

"Shall we go in, Clarke?" His voice came out raspier than usual as he said what he now thought of as his special name for her.

"Anything you say, MacMasters," she replied softly, ready to agree to any of his suggestions.

One of Mac's charm-filled smiles toward the hostess guaranteed them a corner booth overlooking the sea.

"Is there any woman you can't charm?" Jaime demanded after they had ordered their meal. It annoyed her that no woman seemed to have the strength to resist him. She was positive that Mac would have the sensual magic to seduce a woman even when he was eighty!

He picked up her left hand and raised the palm to his lips, then concentrated on nibbling the fingertips. "Yes," he murmured. "But I'm still working on her."

"Mac, you're incorrigible," she whispered, trying to pull her hand away, but he merely tightened his hold.

"No, just hungry for my woman." His eyes twinkled wickedly, letting her know the exact nature of his hunger.

Jaime couldn't halt the fiery shaft that ran through her body when Mac referred to her as his woman. Did he really mean it? She wished she had the courage to ask.

"Mac, darling." She affected a sultry voice. "I need both hands to eat."

"Not if I help you," he offered, only releasing her hand when the waitress arrived with their food.

Jaime was surprised when Mac consulted her regarding which wine to select for dinner. He had even insisted that she taste and approve it when it was served to them.

"I'm a better authority when it comes to beer," he confessed with a rueful grin when she protested this change in roles.

"Who says I'm any better?" she challenged.

There was no mockery in his voice when he replied, "You were brought up to know such things, I wasn't."

Mac's statement aroused Jaime's curiosity about his background, but she still felt reluctant to question him for fear he'd freeze her out of the way he had the first time he mentioned his parentage.

155

How odd, she had shared a bed with this man, had learned to know his body as well as she knew her own, yet she knew next to nothing about his family or childhood.

"Be careful or I might think you have a fixation about my so-called formative years," she said lightly. "Wine tasting isn't even taught at the better schools."

"What was it like at one of those preppy schools?"

Jaime's eyes flew up to study Mac's face. She was positive a bitter mockery edged his question, but there was no trace of the emotion on his bland features, so perhaps she was mistaken.

"I suppose you belonged to a sorority," he continued. "Not to mention the various honor societies."

Jaime sipped her wine slowly, gathering her thoughts together. "I can remember studying until two or three in the morning then sleeping for a few hours before getting up to study again for an exam. I can also remember in my junior year taking my final exams even though I had a temperature of over a hundred. I joined a sorority my mother belonged to for her sake, not because I wanted to. I'm sorry to disappoint you, but I worked hard for every A I got," she said in a clipped tone.

"You enjoy putting me in my place, don't you?" He leaned back in his seat and watched her with narrowed eyes.

"Only when you deserve it."

The tension remained for the balance of the meal and ruined Jaime's appetite. She heaved a silent sigh of relief when they left the restaurant. She could sense the tension in Mac's body when he issued his subtle taunts about her background and wondered what she had done to warrant his attack. She was surprised when, with a resumption of his former good nature, he suggested a walk on the beach.

When they reached the sand, Jaime slipped her shoes off.

Mac draped an arm around her shoulders, drawling, "Come on, old girl."

"Old girl! You make me sound like a dog or a horse!" She

snapped her teeth playfully at him. "Better watch it, buddy. You've got quite a few years on me."

"Ouch!" He winced and hugged her close to his side. "Talk about knowing where to hurt a guy."

They walked along the water's edge in shared silence with arms wrapped around each other's waists. For a brief time, Jaime was able to pretend that Mac was all hers. When he stopped, he turned to face her, his hands resting lightly on her hips. She looked up, barely able to make out his chiseled features in the twilight.

"You're a dangerous woman, Clarke." Mac drew a deep breath. The vibrancy of his dark eyes and the warmth of his smile seemed to reach out to her.

"I've always been a dangerous woman," she murmured, sensing the heat of his body even though a tiny space separated them.

Mac's emotions were in turmoil. There was so much he wanted, and now he couldn't see any way of obtaining his objectives. It had seemed so easy when he first met her. Now he wasn't so confident. Groaning deeply, he hauled her against his chest and wrapped his arms tightly around her.

"Oh, Jaime." His voice was ragged. "I wish to God I was good enough for you. That I could be the kind of man you should have."

She tipped her head back and gazed up with puzzled eyes. "What are you trying to say, Mac?" she demanded. "You sound as if you're trying to belittle yourself to me and I won't let you do that. What do you think is wrong with you? Why do you say these things? You're the finest man I know," she said sincerely.

He pressed her face against his chest and rested his cheek on the top of her head, closing his eyes. He expelled a shuddering breath. He berated himself for doing this to the only woman who was right for him. Why was he pushing her this way? Why did he come on strong, then pull back, only to leave her confused? Easy, he was scared. He was scared that the day would come when Jaime would wake up and realize John MacMasters might

157

be a great lover but he didn't have an impeccable social background. It had never bothered him before. He was a self-made man and damn proud of his accomplishments, but as he listened to Jaime's soft, cultured voice and as he watched the proud way she carried herself, he knew this was a woman who came from a world far different from his own. Around her he forgot just how much he had to offer a woman. She meant much more to him than just a short and satisfying affair. Jaime Clarke meant the world to him.

"So many differences," he murmured, more to himself. "Two different worlds."

Jaime listened to Mac's cryptic words. How would she deal with this? "What am I supposed to do, Mac?" she asked quietly.

"Give me more time," he urged her in a fierce voice.

"Of course," she agreed, still not completely understanding his meaning. She only wondered how much time he would need.

She sensed he was in the midst of some kind of inner battle, a war he would have to fight himself. She ached to help him rid his mind of his torment, but she couldn't. She had her own pain to deal with. The pain of loving a man who would only take her into his bed as long as she pleased him, then blithely move on to greener pastures. Perhaps his self-mockery was to be her warning of what would soon come, the end of their relationship. Until then she would have to take what she could get.

CHAPTER TEN

Jaime swiveled her chair around to look out the window. It was shadowed with a fine mist and silvery water droplets slid down the glass. How fitting the rain was to her pensive mood.

Had it only been a month since Mac's party? Since that night on the beach when he had fought some sort of inner battle? The night he had asked for her understanding and she had given it without hesitation? He had changed so much in the past few weeks that she sometimes wondered if he was the same man she had fallen in love with.

That night they had walked silently back to Mac's car and he had driven her home with almost unseemly haste. After a brief yet painful kiss on the lips, he had left her.

Mac didn't come into the office for the next two days. If Jaime hadn't known that he was embroiled in a problem at the building site, she would have sworn that he was avoiding her. Then, the following day, Mac strolled into the office and buzzed Jaime. Would she care to go to dinner with him that Friday evening? She didn't hesitate before saying yes to his almost formal invitation.

"I'll have Sue make reservations," he had told her before hanging up.

Jaime was stunned. The quietly elegant restaurant he had mentioned wasn't what she expected for one of their evenings.

Determined to look her best, she left the office early that Friday to keep a hair and manicure appointment.

A trim of the feathered ends of her hair left them lying silkily on her nape and cheeks, and the melon polish brushed on her nails was a perfect complement to the lemon silk sheath with narrow straps and closely fitted bodice she had chosen to wear that evening. As she stroked on perfume, her nerve endings quivered with anticipation. It hadn't taken her long to realize that her body hungered for Mac's touch. No, it was more than that; she *required* his touch as strongly as she needed air to breathe. She stroked the spicy scent in the cleft between her breasts, wishing the perfume could weave some magic spell that would make him hers forever.

A new Mac greeted Jaime that night. His charcoal three-piece suit fitted his body perfectly and he looked as comfortable in it as if he had worn a suit every day of his life. Though she sensed that deep down he felt very unused to such fine clothes, it didn't show in his demeanor. Even his dark hair had been suitably tamed.

His face betrayed no emotion when she opened the door, although for one brief moment a flash burned in his eyes.

"Shall we go?" He assisted her with her coat, as impersonally as if she were a casual acquaintance, then escorted her outside to his car.

Jaime remained bewildered all through dinner. She wasn't sure about this new Mac she was seeing. She was well enough acquainted with his tastes to know that this exclusive restaurant wasn't what he would readily choose, and she loved him too much to tell him it wasn't the kind she would choose either. For some reason he was making a special effort just for her. Only time would tell her why.

That evening Mac was formal and correct, his speech quiet, his manner commanding yet differential to her. There was nothing of the earthy, virile, and loving man she had lost her heart to and Jaime found herself missing him desperately.

"You're quiet tonight," Mac commented after they had

finished dinner. He sat in his chair sipping his brandy and watching her closely.

Jaime smiled faintly, dipping her head. Her fingertip idly circled the rim of her glass as she searched for the proper words to reveal her confusion. "Dinner was excellent," she murmured, still evading the little voice prompting her to speak her thoughts.

"Perhaps you'd care to go dancing somewhere?" He seemed unaware of her troubled mind, as if he had suddenly lost the knack of reading her thoughts.

"I don't know if I could move." She injected a light note, all the while wanting nothing more than his arms around her, his lips moving over her bare skin, his— She drew a swift breath. Perhaps this was what was needed. Trembling fingers moved away from the glass. "Why not?" The brandy was beginning to make her feel reckless.

Jaime was doomed to disappointment. While she found it difficult to think rationally with Mac's arms around her, he didn't seem to have the same problem. Moving slowly in time to the music, his thighs brushed hers through the thin silk of her dress. She linked her arms around his neck, the top of her head just brushing his chin. There was nothing in Mac's manner that indicated he was as affected by Jaime as she was by him.

They stayed at the club until it closed. Then Mac took her directly home.

"Would you like to come in for coffee?" Jaime asked, silently cursing herself for not having a more novel way of inviting him in. She stood to one side as Mac took her keys and inserted the correct one in the lock.

"Thanks, but I've got to be up early tomorrow." He opened the door and handed her the keys. "Good night, Jaime, I'll see you Monday." His kiss was warm but held none of his usual passion. It gave no hint of anything more to come. Jaime's lips automatically parted when his firm mouth covered hers, but he didn't accept the provocative invitation. "Sleep well." Was there a husky note not usually in his voice or was it just wishful thinking on her part?

Jaime undressed and slipped on a nightgown, then carefully removed her makeup and applied a light moisturizer. She didn't sleep at all that night; her mind raced frantically for an answer. Nothing made sense.

Just after dawn Jaime picked up her phone and dialed a number. Ignoring Karla's grumblings and reminder of the early hour, she made a tennis date for later that morning. As Karla argued with her about the insanity of playing tennis on such a cold morning, Jaime quietly hung up.

Her frustrations were partially eased on the tennis court. Dressed in white shorts and a thin pullover sweater, she was a figure of pure energy on the court.

"Hold it! No more!" Karla held her two arms up in surrender. "Have a heart, Jaime, you're killing me! Wouldn't it be easier if you just told me what's bothering you?" She walked slowly over to the bench next to the fence and picked up a towel to mop her perspiring face.

"I don't know what you're talking about," Jaime replied, picking up her racquet cover and zipping it around the racquet. "I was in the mood to play and decided to give you a call. I didn't realize it was a crime to call a friend."

"Only when you call me at six in the morning. Neil and I drove to L.A. last night to see a movie. Then we ran into some old friends. We didn't get home until two and then, of course, there was your oh-so-charming call just four short hours later. It certainly didn't help to watch his highness fall blissfully back to sleep when I crawled out of bed a couple of hours ago either," Karla informed her dryly, putting away her own racquet and dropping the yellow balls in a can. "Look, how about some breakfast? My battered body could use a little nourishment at this point." She grimaced as she stretched her arms over her head and found a sore muscle.

Strangely, Jaime's distraught mood didn't interfere with her appetite. Karla sat back in her chair and marveled at the hearty breakfast her friend consumed.

"When I discovered I was in love with Neil, I couldn't eat solid food for almost a week," she observed a little sarcastically.

Jaime flushed as she chewed the last bite of her butter-topped muffin. "Then I guess I'm not in love," she muttered, looking down at her empty plate.

"Oh, sure." Karla shook her head in disbelief. "It won't work, Jaime, I've known you too long and have seen how you've handled men in the past. You've fallen for your boss, haven't you?" she pressed.

Jaime's face paled. "And if I say yes, will the hurt go away?" she asked between stiff lips. "Will I be able to sleep at night, or is my world still going to fall down around my ears?" She blinked back the tears beginning to form.

Karla sighed sympathetically. Why did love have to be so complicated?

"No matter what happens, the sun will still come up in the east and set in the west, the desert won't fall into the ocean, and life will go on just the way it has for thousands of years," she replied quietly. "And you'll go on living, much wiser for the experience. Are you really so sure he doesn't care for you? Jaime, I saw the way he looked at you that day in the restaurant parking lot. Frankly, his thoughts might have been on tossing you into the nearest bed but there was also a tenderness in his expression that had nothing to do with lust."

Jaime shook her head. "I don't know," she confessed, shrugging her shoulders. She then went on to tell Karla the entire story, even about Mac asking her for more time, that he needed to think things out.

"Then give it to him," Karla urged. "You'd be a fool if you didn't. It will all work out, you'll see."

"I hope so." Jaime sighed. "I really hope so."

* * *

In the weeks that followed, Jaime went out with Mac often. They usually went to dinner and then to a concert or play or dancing. There was never anything in Mac's manner to indicate they had been lovers. The touch of his hand on her arm, the cool press of his lips on hers, only led up to a bitter frustration for Jaime. She was ready to scream out a demand to know why he had changed. She was also beginning to wonder if she should bother hanging around any longer. She knew breaking up with Mac would be terribly painful, but perhaps she should do it now before the sorrow became unbearable.

"Have you noticed a change in Mac lately?" Sue asked Jaime one afternoon when they went out to lunch to a nearby coffee shop.

She ducked her head to study the sandwich she had ordered. "He seems the same to me," she mumbled.

Sue shook her head. "No, something's going on." She gazed intently at Jaime. "The two of you go out quite a bit. You must notice *something* unusual," she persisted.

"I think he's just been working too hard what with the ground-breaking soon on the Royalton job." She knew she had to come up with something before Sue began to dig too deep. As it was, Jaime didn't have any more of an idea than the secretary did. "You know how Mac can be when things aren't done just his way."

"Well, I think you better have a talk with him because he's overdoing it, and if he keeps it up, we'll have a walking zombie on our hands," she declared.

Jaime nodded, all the while feeling that she didn't have the right to say anything to Mac just now. Not until they got things straightened out between them—if they ever did.

When Mac suggested attending a concert at Irvine Meadows that Saturday evening, Jaime countered with the suggestion of cooking dinner at her house.

"Maybe if I get him drunk, I could seduce him," she muttered to herself.

When Saturday night came, Jaime chose an emerald-green silky jumpsuit that left nothing to the imagination. In the past few weeks, she had found herself shopping for clothes meant to titillate the senses. By now she was frantic to do anything to catch his attention.

"If this doesn't do it, nothing will." She surveyed her reflection in the mirror just as the doorbell rang. She took a deep breath and lowered the zipper another inch, revealing the curving sides of her bare breasts.

Mac's eyes widened slightly at the blatant picture Jaime presented, but merely said he had brought a bottle of wine to go with dinner. He said nothing about her provocative outfit.

"Wonderful," Jaime said a shade too brightly. "I hope you like spicy food. When I make lasagna, I tend to get a little heavy-handed with the oregano."

"I'm sure it's great," Mac assured her.

She hurried into the kitchen, wishing she could have the privacy to sit down for a good cry. Why were things so strained between them? She took a deep breath and silently wondered what kind of aphrodisiac goes with Italian food. Wishing she knew of one, she picked up the pot holders and opened the oven door.

Dinner was equally stilted. Their polite conversation might have been between two strangers. Blind dates had been more interesting, Jaime thought ruefully. By the end of the meal, it took all of her self-control not to burst into tears. She refused Mac's offer to help with the dishes and merely stacked them in the sink. It would give her something to do later that night instead of walking the floor racking her brain to find the cause of Mac's strange behavior.

When Jaime returned to the living room, she found Mac prowling around, a filled wineglass in one hand. She could see raw pain etched in his face. Jaime stood in the doorway, her hands clenched in front of her.

"Mac, what's wrong?" she pleaded with him. "Is it the project? Are you having problems with it? Surely you know you can talk about it with me. Talk about anything. Please, say something!" Her voice rose with her agitation.

He shook his head slowly as he walked over to a nearby chair and sat down. "I've been doing a lot of thinking, Jaime, and it just isn't going to work," he said bleakly, looking down at his wineglass.

She experienced a choking sensation and had to grab onto the doorway for fear her legs would give out from under her. "What won't work?" She was finally able to force the words past suddenly cold lips.

"Us." Mac's shoulders settled in a weary slump. "I've tried, Jaime, I really have, but I don't fit in your world. I guess you'd say I'm too rough around the edges. I don't have the education and I certainly don't have the polish," he finished derisively.

The answers were starting to come in loud and clear. "Is this why we've been going to all those concerts and plays?" she asked him. "Because you thought that's what I would prefer to do? Did you think you needed to impress me?"

Mac nodded. "I thought I could show you that I could take you to the same places other men took you to. I'm sorry, it just isn't me. Everywhere we went, you looked as if you belonged there while I felt as if I was there on a pass. You belong with people like that, I don't." He leaned forward and set his glass on the coffee table and muttered, "Hell, I even hate wine."

"You never needed to impress me, Mac," she choked, walking unsteadily to the couch. "I never cared where we went as long as I was with you."

Mac slowly raised his head. "Sue once told me you were out of my league, but I didn't want to believe her. Now I can see she was right." Pain swiftly flickered across his face, then disappeared. "I think we should end it before it gets any worse."

Jaime's hand shook violently as she leaned forward to set her glass on the table. "End it." She vainly tried to swallow the lump in her throat. "Do you mean end everything?"

166

"It's the only way."

"Is it?" she demanded, clenching her fists in her lap. "All I ever cared about was being with you, Mac. Nothing else mattered, even though it appears it did with you. For someone who always seemed to be able to read my mind, you seem to be terribly remiss in certain areas."

"I'm only a novelty to you right now, Jaime. I'm thirty-seven years old and I'm still going to school. Damn it, I'm old enough to be the father to some of the kids in my classes!" he gritted, shaking his head as if to clear the cobwebs. "I go to school three nights a week and study every spare moment I have because it takes more time to cram the facts into my thick head."

"Did you ever think about letting someone help you?" she volunteered softly. She didn't want to tell him that she already knew about his return to school. That would always remain a secret. What hurt was that Mac hadn't thought enough of her to tell her about his classes. "You can't remain alone forever. You have to allow someone into your life. That's what you were doing with me. You were pulling me out of my sugarcoated existence and letting me see life the way it really was. Why won't you let me stay?"

Mac jumped to his feet and walked over to where Jaime sat. Leaning over, he placed a hand on either side of the couch back so she would be forced to stay and hear his harsh words. "You're a beautiful woman, Jaime, and you're warm and caring, but I won't take your pity," he told her quietly. "I'm sorry, God, how I'm sorry. I only wish there was a way, but there isn't. I don't want you to wake up some morning and realize what a mistake you made in tying up with a nobody like me."

All the time he spoke, she stared into his eyes, hypnotized by the purple orbs. It took a moment for her to realize he had straightened up and was walking to the door. Jaime stood up, her body stiff with an inner rage. She wasn't as angry at the man as she was with his pride.

"You're so blind, MacMasters." Her voice shook with the

violent emotions she felt. "Did you really think I would be that shallow? If so, then you don't know me as well as you thought you did. For some reason, you're running scared. I think you're afraid of losing me. I don't know, maybe a girl did just that to you years ago and you vowed that another woman wouldn't ever get that close. *You* were the one who chased after me in the beginning! *You* were the one who became my lover. Well, buddy, I have some news for you. I love you, you stupid, crazy man."

His hand froze on the doorknob for a moment as her words sunk in. Then he slowly turned the knob and pulled the door open.

"I love you and I want to be everything to you, including your friend."

Mac's harsh laugh cut her to the bone. "Baby, we can never be friends. That word just doesn't fit into our vocabulary." He walked out the door and closed it behind him.

Jaime stood there, now beyond tears or anger. She was totally numb from shock that Mac could so casually end their relationship. She had even gone so far as to confess her love for him and he had only thrown it back in her face! She refused to recognize the agony in his voice or the pain etched on his face.

"If he thinks I'm going to calmly exit from his life, he has another think coming." There was a grim determination in her voice. "I'm not finished, not by any means, John MacMasters. You broke down all my barriers. Well, now it's your turn. I'm going to haunt you at every turn until you admit you need me."

Jaime's determination was even stronger by Monday. She had refused to sit around and mope all day Sunday and cleaned out all her closets to get rid of some of her excess energy. She still couldn't believe that Mac felt he was better off without her.

Monday morning was difficult for her. She did her best to act as if nothing were wrong, but she felt as if her life were over. She thought the morning would never end.

"Did you and Mac have an argument?" Sue asked her when they met for lunch that day.

Jaime toyed idly with her spinach salad, wishing she hadn't ordered it. "No, why?"

"I've never seen the man in such a foul mood as he is today." She shuddered. "Jaime, it's positively scary. I can't remember ever seeing him like this. Maybe you can corner him this afternoon and kiss him into a better mood."

"I doubt that it would work," she murmured, refusing to confess the real reason for Mac's bad mood. She kept her head down, avoiding Sue's puzzled expression.

When Jaime returned from lunch, she was surprised to find a note on her desk asking that she come to Mac's office.

Wiping clammy palms on her coffee-color wool pants, she left her office after telling Gina she'd be back in a few moments.

When Jaime entered Mac's office, she first noticed that he looked as haggard as she felt. He looked up and gestured for her to take a seat before he began to speak.

"I'm afraid we have a problem here," he began gruffly, not looking at her as he studied the pen he was twirling between his thumb and fingers.

"Oh?" She straightened her shoulders.

"I just don't feel we can work to our best abilities under the present conditions," he continued.

"A situation of *your* making, not mine," Jaime reminded him in a cool voice, while hurting inside. Would they always be at odds with each other now? What about the times they shared together, the love? Didn't that mean anything to him?

Mac exhaled a heavy sigh. He refused to look at Jaime for fear he'd undo what he had begun and needed to finish. He knew he was doing what was right even though the hurt would last his lifetime.

"Either way, it can't go on." He hesitated. "To be blunt, I think it would be better all the way around if you didn't work here any longer."

Jaime sat frozen in her chair. "Are—" She stopped, unable to form the words. "Are you firing me?"

"No!" he argued hoarsely, looking up with pain-filled eyes. "I'll accept your resignation and I'll certainly give you an excellent reference."

"Saying what?" she demanded, swallowing to keep back the tears. "Not only that I am an excellent accountant, but a great lay," she finished crudely.

Mac's eyes flashed at her choice of words. He looked as if he would like nothing better than to shake her senseless. "You can just say you preferred to work in a larger company," he said bleakly.

"No!" Jaime grated, leaning forward in her chair. "Oh, no, I'm not going to allow you to make the biggest mistake of your life. I'm perfectly happy here, there are no complaints about my work, and here I'll stay." Her mouth was set in stubborn lines.

"Jaime, you're only making matters worse." His husky voice tore at her heart.

"Why, will I be some kind of embarrassment when your little blond girl friends start showing up again?" she argued vehemently.

"It's for the best."

"Like hell," she snarled, totally unlike her usually composed self. "You're the one calling it quits, Mac, not me. You're the one who refuses to see how good we are together. Why am I so wrong all of a sudden?" she asked in a pleading voice.

Mac shook his head slowly. "Look at us, Jaime. You with your college education and I'm still struggling for my degree. You've grown up with the best of everything while I was lucky to own more than a few pair of jeans. You drive an expensive car and think nothing of it; wear designer clothes and don't consider the cost; can go to any fancy restaurant around here and they know you by name." Deep lines were etched around his mouth. "Oh, I admit you aren't spoiled, but our backgrounds are miles apart and just can't be joined up."

Jaime couldn't stop the tears from filling her eyes. "You're so wrong, Mac," she whispered, shaking her head. "If only I could make you see that, but for some reason you refuse to listen. I won't resign. It isn't fair to ask me to."

A muscle twitched in the corner of his mouth and his face betrayed his haunted state. Mac stood up and placed his palms on top of the desk to brace himself. He suddenly looked older than his thirty-seven years, and it hurt her to see him this way. "Please don't make this harder on the both of us."

She tossed her head in sudden defiance. "What will you do if I won't quit, fire me?" she taunted in a bitter voice.

"Yes." Without hesitation.

That one word was enough to drain all of the color out of Jaime's face. A search of Mac's features told her he meant it and his next words were further proof.

"I'd appreciate it if you'd clean your desk out and be gone by the end of the day." His words were almost too painful to bear.

"You're a fool, John MacMasters." Jaime spoke with a deadly calm. "I only wish I knew the words to make you believe me. The day will come when you'll find out exactly how big a mistake you've made. There's not all that much in my desk, so I'll be gone within the hour." She turned and walked out of the office with the regal bearing of a queen. If she had turned around, she would have seen Mac slump down in his chair and bury his face in his hands.

As Jaime hurriedly cleared her desk of personal possessions, Sue walked in. The older woman surveyed her tear-stained face and jerky movements and knew she didn't need any explanation.

"You quit, didn't you?" she stated.

"Quit?" Jaime laughed bitterly. "I was fired."

"Fired?" Sue's eyes widened in surprise. "But I thought—we hoped—"

"Didn't we all?" she gritted. "No, he fired me because he's looking out for my best interests, and if you can figure that one out, you're doing a hell of a lot better than I am."

Jaime opened the top desk drawer and withdrew a checkbook. Mac had asked her to reconcile his personal account and she had intended to give it back to him that morning. Part of her was tempted to give it to Sue to return it, while the other part told her not to be a coward. She slammed the drawer shut.

"One more thing and I'll be gone." She slapped the checkbook against her open palm.

Jaime climbed the stairs and walked into Mac's office without knocking. He looked up with surprise, then slowly flipped on the speaker phone.

"Yes, Sue?" He didn't bother to acknowledge Jaime's presence.

"Louise is on line two. Shall I tell her you're busy?"

He raised his head, looking her squarely in the eye. "No, I'll take it." He punched the appropriate button. His voice had that low, sexy drawl Jaime knew so well. "Hi, lovely lady, where have you been?"

"Me!" A woman's husky contralto came out a little distorted, yet still sinfully sexy, over the speaker phone. "Mac, you're the one who hasn't called in weeks. I hope that you don't mind my calling you at work."

"Of course not. I'm afraid I've been busy on a new project lately." Mac still ignored Jaime as she silently laid the checkbook on the desk and stepped back a pace. "What can I do for you?" he asked in a low, sexy voice.

The woman's laugh revealed more than words. "Talk about a loaded question. To tell you the truth, I've missed you and thought you might be free for dinner and"—she paused delicately—"conversation this evening."

Mac's eyes were positively glacial as he leaned back in his chair and stared at Jaime. "Sounds good to me. Especially the latter," he drawled.

For the first time since all this began, Jaime's eyes filled with angry, hot tears. Her low whisper barely reached his ears. "You bastard—" She bit down hard on her lower lip. "Fine, go back

172

to a woman who might be able to carry on an intelligent 'conversation,' but just remember one thing. I never asked you to change for me, that was your idea. I love you the way you are. Just remember that when you're gray and still looking for the right woman. Just remember that *you* were the one to destroy a good thing." She whirled around and slammed the door shut after her.

"Mac?" Louise's curious voice brought him back to the present. "Is someone there with you? What's going on there?"

"I have to go, Louise. On second thought, I won't be free tonight. I'll call you," he said abruptly, depressing the button on her high-pitched voice and leaving behind a heavy silence.

When Sue entered Mac's office late that afternoon, she found him slumped in his chair staring morosely out the window.

"Why did you do it, Mac?" she asked softly. "Why did you destroy her that way?"

He shook his head slowly. "I had to do it before she left me, Sue," he said bleakly. "And the day would have come when she would do just that. You said so yourself."

She walked over and pressed her hands on his shoulders. "I was wrong about her. She was the best thing that ever came into your life," she stated. "I'm just sorry you treated her the way you did. I only hope you'll be able to live with yourself after this."

He sighed wearily. "Exist maybe, but it'll be a long time before I'm able to live again."

Sue patted his shoulder and walked out of the office. She knew he needed to be alone. She silently prayed he would come to his senses before it became far too late.

CHAPTER ELEVEN

Jaime had no desire to find a new job. Instead, she registered with several temporary employment agencies. Right now, she preferred to stay with companies a short time and move on. She kept to herself, not caring to make any new friends, and she kindly but firmly rebuffed all overtures from men.

Her mother had left on her cruise the week before. It had been hard for Jaime to hide the fact that she was jobless from the older woman, but she hadn't wanted anything to mar her trip. Perhaps by the time Eileen returned Jaime would be more like her old self. Perhaps.

Jaime lost weight she couldn't afford, and sleep was a thing of the past. She dreamed about Mac every night. The memory of his lovemaking and fierce yet gentle possession now tormented her.

Sue called her several times and suggested they meet for lunch, but Jaime put her off with vague, unconvincing excuses. It would be a long time before she would be able to live with her pain, and she wanted no reminders just yet.

Jaime stared again at the engraved invitation to Gina's wedding lying on her dresser. A note had been inserted with a sincere plea that she attend.

She closed her eyes, recalling the night they had celebrated Gina's engagement. Mac's arms around her while they danced, his mouth searing hers later that night . . .

174

"No!" she whispered fiercely, willing the memories to disappear. "No more!"

Jaime was sorely tempted not to attend the wedding, but Sue had called her the evening before and persuaded her to go, saying she and Ray would pick her up.

"Gina is looking forward to seeing you, Jaime," Sue told her. "We all are."

"Is Mac going to be there?" she asked bluntly. Funny, his name wasn't as hard to say as she thought it would be.

"He said he wasn't going," she replied. "Something about weddings not being his idea of fun."

Of course not, Jaime thought sorrowfully. That isn't his style. She closed her eyes and placed the telephone receiver briefly against her forehead in thought, then replaced it to her ear. At least she wouldn't have to face Mac with another woman in tow. "What time will you pick me up?" she asked with a sigh.

The next morning she was out early to purchase a present and a new dress that would suit the occasion.

As she dressed for the wedding, she knew she had made a wise choice. The soft peach silk added color to her pale cheeks and the handkerchief hem swirled silkily around her legs. Even more careful makeup couldn't add a fullness to her cheeks, but it did detract from her pallor. After brushing her hair into soft swirls around her head, she stroked on perfume. She had just finished applying a peachy lip gloss when her doorbell rang.

"Hm, they're early," Jaime murmured, switching on a bright smile as she went to the door. A smile that faltered, then disappeared when she opened the door to a somber-faced Mac. Her hand gripped the edge of the door as if to slam it shut.

"Hello, Jaime." His voice was unusually quiet, his eyes silently pleading with her not to shut the door on him.

"What are you doing here?" she gasped, experiencing all the pain returning in fierce waves. "I should think you wouldn't care to come back here again. We're a mistake, remember?" she jeered, wanting him to feel as much pain as she did.

Mac flinched at her bitter words. "Could I come in?"

"I don't think so. I'm waiting for Sue and Ray to pick me up for Gina's wedding. They'll be here any minute." Her voice was cool and distant.

"I know. Sue called and asked me if I would mind picking you up since they're running late."

"She said you weren't going!" Jaime wasn't sure whom she was accusing, adding in a scathing tone, "I believe it was something about weddings not being your style."

Mac's face was etched with deep furrows, lines carved deep from nose to mouth. Was there even more silver than before scattered through the unruly dark hair? He looked so tired!

"So that's why you agreed to go." He spoke more to himself. "You thought I wouldn't be there."

Something about his quiet acceptance tore at Jaime's heart. "I'll get my purse," she murmured, turning away.

From her bedroom, Jaime could watch Mac without his seeing her. His pearl-gray suit seemed a little loose on him. It wasn't difficult to tell that he had also lost weight. If she didn't know better, she'd swear these past weeks had been just as hard on him as they had been on her.

Mac turned as she walked back into the living room. "You look lovely," he murmured, watching her with dark, hungry eyes.

She ducked her head, feeling a little uncomfortable with this new, strangely quiet Mac. "Thank you." She turned around swiftly to pick up the wedding gift before she succumbed to his compelling eyes. Once outside, she was glad for the cool spring air caressing her heated cheeks.

Conversation was stilted during the short drive to the chapel.

"I understand you've been working at Watson Land Development for the past few weeks," Mac commented casually.

Jaime shot him a sharp glance. "Where did you hear that?" she asked tightly, then answered her own question. "Sue."

He nodded. "She'd drop little bits and pieces every now and

then about your jobs." He turned his head and looked at her briefly. "I'm surprised that with your qualifications, you didn't get snapped up right away."

"I didn't want a permanent job," she replied tautly.

"Have you been doing well?"

"Well enough." She couldn't resist asking. "Did you find another accountant?"

Mac shook his head. "Royalton keeps me too busy to worry about finding a replacement. The girls are doing a good enough job on their own."

Jaime felt a little hurt that he could so easily dismiss her position. She hadn't realized she was that dispensable. She had been surprised to hear of his knowledge of her temporary jobs. Why would he care about keeping track of her? Her thoughts were diverted by the sight of the chapel ahead of them.

The chapel was situated on bluffs overlooking the ocean. Many of the guests had already arrived and were standing outside on the lawn enjoying the warm spring sunshine before going into the dim confines of the church. It didn't take Jaime and Mac long to find Sue and Ray standing near the entrance. Sue's smile was broad when she greeted them although Jaime could see concern in her eyes.

"You planned this," Jaime accused under her breath.

"Yes, and I think it's going quite well." She showed no signs of guilt.

Seated next to Mac in the church pew, Jaime was intensely aware of him. Neither of them could move without brushing against the other.

The strains of the Wedding March poured out, and the guests stood to watch the bride's progress down the aisle. Gina's smile was radiant as she walked down to her very-soon-to-be husband.

Jaime's eyes filled with tears as the couple recited their vows. A hand covered hers and gave it a reassuring squeeze, which she unconsciously returned. At the same time a handkerchief was pressed into her other hand.

"Crying is allowed at weddings." Mac turned his head to murmur in her ear.

"I'm not crying." She sniffed, lifting the handkerchief to her eyes. "I have something in my eye." She didn't protest when Mac's arms circled her shoulders, keeping her close to his side.

"Oh, Jaime, I'm so glad you came!" Gina bubbled over when Jaime and Mac appeared before her in the reception line. "I'd like you to meet Alan." Her face was glowing when she looked up at her new husband. A love-filled gaze that tore through Jaime's heart. She envied Gina so much!

Jaime sipped the champagne Mac brought her, nibbled a few bites of wedding cake, and smiled and spoke when necessary. Only if someone cared to look deeper could they see how strained her smile was and the torment in her clouded eyes.

"Shall we dance?" Mac asked.

She looked up unable to believe her ears. "All right," she agreed with some reluctance. It was going to be hard enough to go back to her solitary existence as it was.

Mac clasped her around the waist so that she had no choice but to lift her arms and to circle his neck. In this far from impersonal embrace, she could detect the hint of his cologne mingling with the musky scent of his skin, an added stimulant to the senses. Her mind raced madly to think of anything besides the potent attraction of Mac's body brushing warmly against hers.

"Don't shut me out, Jaime." His murmur warmed the sensitive skin by the temple. "God, anything but that."

"Shouldn't I?" She couldn't lie to him. He'd see through it in no time. He still had free access to her mind. "You were the one who shut me out, remember?"

He exhaled sharply at her bitter accusation. There was no retort because he knew she was right. "There was a reason," he replied wearily.

Jaime drew back and looked up at him. Her sparkling eyes brimmed with tears.

"No more, Mac," she whispered her aching plea. "Please, I just can't take any more." Suppressing her sob, she broke away and fled to the ladies' room.

Grateful to find it unoccupied, she indulged herself in a good but short cry. The tears had been building up inside ever since all of this first started. After she regained control of herself, she pressed a damp towel to her hot cheeks and reddened eyes, knowing it wouldn't really help. For now, her main thought was looking for a telephone and calling for a taxi. She needed to get away from Mac before she broke down in front of him. Dancing with him had been too close a call for her peace of mind.

Jaime found a pay telephone just outside the ladies' room and quickly made her call, grateful to hear a taxi could be there in a few minutes. She carefully made her way to the exit and breathed a sigh of relief when she didn't see Mac.

She waited outside until the taxi pulled up. She was just telling the driver where to take her, when a hand settled on her shoulder and gently pulled her back.

"Oh!" She looked up, fearing the worst when she saw the anger flaring in Mac's eyes.

A muscle twitched in the corner of his mouth as he looked down at her shimmering eyes and trembling mouth. Mac leaned down and said something to the driver, handing him a folded bill. Jaime stood woodenly beside him and watched her hope of escape drive away. Without saying a word, he propelled her inside and down the hallway, keeping them away from the reception guests. He pushed her around a corner and flat against a wall, pressing his body intimately against hers. He was determined that she wouldn't escape him this time.

"God, Jaime, what you do to me," he rasped, dipping his head toward hers.

"Don't, Mac," she pleaded tearfully, while her entire body was burning for his touch. "You should have let me leave with the taxi and let it end there. I mean it, I just can't take any more." She sobbed, now not caring that he saw her tears.

179

"I hurt too," he said, his lips a fraction of an inch from hers. "I hurt because I still remember the feel of your body against mine, your hands and lips loving me and me loving you back. You've cast a spell on me, you little witch," he accused hoarsely.

"I—I don't know what you mean," she faltered, every nerve vitally aware of his strength.

"I wanted to forget you and the only way I could was with other women." The fire in his eyes threatened to consume her. Her face paled as the meaning of his words sunk in and she could feel a violent nausea rising in her throat. How could he hurt her more by telling this? "But I couldn't," he ground out, his face gray beneath his tan as he reached out to grasp her forearms with rough fingertips. "I couldn't do a damn thing. All because of you."

At that moment Jaime wasn't sure whether she wanted to lash out at him in anger or laugh hysterically at his heated accusation.

"I'm surprised that Louise didn't have the experience to help you with your problem," she spat out sarcastically. She vainly tried to push past him, but he wasn't ready to let her go just yet. "You said she was a more than capable woman."

Mac's features hardened under her words. "Oh, no, Clarke," he breathed, dipping his head to nuzzle her throat and find the rapidly beating pulse. "There've been too many words between us before. We should have learned by now that we're better off with actions."

"No!" Jaime cried out just as his mouth covered hers, his plunging tongue exploring the honeyed sweetness in the moist caverns of her mouth. Her body trembled as his hands drifted down to her hips to draw her closer to him.

"You were right, I am stupid." Mac's admission came out in a ragged voice when he tore his mouth from hers. He thrust his hips gently at her, wanting her to know just how badly he needed her. "You know me better than I know myself. My pride almost destroyed us, but I'm not going to allow that to happen again.

This time everything is going to be the way it should have in the beginning."

"No more empty promises!" She tried to push him away. "I was just starting to get over you. I won't let you hurt me again. I was just barely able to pick up the pieces this time."

He drew an uneven breath and reached down to take her hand and place it against his chest, allowing her to feel the rapid race of his heart by sliding her fingers between the buttons of his shirt. "If I have to convince you of my sincerity, I'd prefer doing it in more private surroundings."

"I'd rather be taken home and left alone," Jaime cried, swiftly withdrawing her hand as if she had been burned.

He thought for a moment then nodded his head. It was useless to argue with her. "All right, I'll take you home," he said quietly, moving back to allow her to pass him.

The drive to Jaime's house was silent. She wondered if she should dare to listen to Mac's explanation, but she wasn't sure she could survive another shock like the last one. At the same time, her heart told her that if Mac was sincere and she didn't give him a chance to speak, she'd never forgive herself. She had taken a chance falling in love with him. It looks as if she would have to take another chance to see if she could keep him.

"I have some steaks in the freezer if you're feeling a little hungry." She offered a truce hesitantly, when Mac parked his car in front of her house. "They wouldn't take long to fix."

Surprised by her invitation, Mac turned his head and studied her for a long moment. "Are you sure it isn't any trouble?"

She nodded. "Positive."

Inside the house, Jaime motioned for him to take a seat. She slipped her shoes off and placed them by a chair before she went into the kitchen.

"There's bourbon in the liquor cabinet if you want a drink," she told him while she took the steaks out of the freezer and stuck them in the microwave to defrost.

181

"Would you like something?" he asked as she heard the click of the cabinet door opening.

"Not just yet." She quickly surveyed her refrigerator contents for salad makings.

Jaime quickly fixed a green salad and baked potatoes to go with the steaks. All the time she worked, her jittery nerves reminded her of the man in her living room. Could she be content with just this one evening, knowing Mac would later walk out the door and she probably wouldn't see him again?

She knew what he really wanted. He wanted to make love to her and get her out of his system once and for all so that he could get on with his life. Could she allow him to do that, or would it leave an even deeper mark in her heart? She took a deep breath before walking out to the living room and informing him that dinner was ready.

Mac was surprised by the hearty dinner Jaime had prepared in such a short time and told her so.

"Having the microwave helps. Besides, I like to cook. I just don't do it as much as I should." She felt warmed by his praise.

Remembering Mac's distaste for wine, she served coffee with their meal. Talk was desultory, mainly comments about the wedding. Jaime felt as if he was deliberately skirting the real issue. She was still confused by the things he had said at the reception hall. She wasn't allowed to wonder any more when Mac insisted on helping her with the dishes and clean up the kitchen. Now, minus his suit coat and tie with his shirt sleeves rolled up to his elbows, he looked more relaxed than she had seen him in a long time. He was the Mac she had fallen in love with.

She wasn't even aware of his skillfully steering her into the living room and seating her on the couch until it was too late. Mac fixed himself another bourbon, but Jaime refused his offer to fix her a drink. She needed to keep her head clear for his conversation. He then sat in the easy chair across from her.

"I guess we have some things to talk out," Mac said in a low voice, refusing to look at her just then. "Things kind of got out of hand at our last meeting."

Jaime stiffened, remembering the day Mac fired her and his conversation with Louise. "More like the truth coming to the surface." Her voice cooled. "I hadn't realized how fond you were of Louise."

Mac had the grace to wince. "I deserved that." He took a hearty swallow of his drink. "It's pretty tame compared to what I've thought of myself since then, not to mention what Sue and the others have been calling me. No matter what you think of me, I did what I had to do for your sake."

"*My* sake?" Jaime arched a disbelieving eyebrow. "Oh, please don't do me any more favors," she said bitterly.

He lifted the glass to his lips, grimaced, then set it down on the table. "I seem to be doing a lot of this lately. Shall we set the record straight?"

"By all means."

Mac took a deep breath and leaned forward, resting his forearms on his spread thighs. "You were right, Jaime, I am in love with you. I'm so in love with you that I can't even think straight. I can't remember the last time I've slept more than an hour or two at night."

"You certainly can't blame me for your lack of energy." She wasn't about to hide her bitterness at the thought that he might have found someone else to share his bed—the bed he claimed no woman before her had ever shared.

Mac's temper was beginning to rise. "If you'd shut up and listen for a few minutes, I'm sure you'd learn what you want to know. This is what you've wanted all along, isn't it?" His words had a caustic bite to them.

Jaime flushed, but she refused to back down. "You said that you finally realized you loved me. When? This afternoon when you came to pick me up? Or was it tonight over dinner? I can't believe it was before that. Oh, *I* knew you loved me. I've known

183

it for a long time. But I was beginning to think you'd never figure it out."

"A man has his pride, Jaime." He exhaled a deep breath. "I also still felt I was staying away from you for your own good."

"My own good!" She pressed her fingertips against her forehead, willing the pain to disappear. "I can't see where you thought you were helping me."

Mac raised his eyes, now a dark, glowing purple, his mouth twisted in a wry smile. "You are the most exasperating woman I've ever met, Clarke. I began falling in love with you the day I interviewed you. I even told Sue I was going to marry you before the year was out, but she thought I was crazy. I knew my feelings were right that night we first made love and I discovered that you had given me a beautiful gift—yourself. It didn't help when you allowed me to think you were sleeping with what's 'is name either," he growled.

Jaime smiled. Deep down, Neil was still bothering Mac even after meeting Karla and seeing the obvious love between the two.

"Finding out you hadn't slept with him threw me a curve. It also made you very precious to me. I do love you, Jaime, but I don't know if that will be enough for you. You can say what you want about it, but we do come from different backgrounds. There are still a lot of people in this world who think that is very important."

"Oh, Mac." She sighed, feeling a familiar warmth steal through her body. "You're making it sound like a melodrama. The main difference between us is that you're a man and I'm a woman. I certainly don't see anything wrong with that." She managed a faint smile.

"No, Jaime we're very different; you can't deny it. I like country-and-western music, you go more for the classics; I like steak and chili dogs, you enjoy French food; I drink bourbon and beer, you drink wine." He slowly raised his eyes and looked at her squarely. "You once offered your services as a tutor. How would you feel about teaching some ignorant lout the finer things in life?" he added wryly. "We'll talk about a few of my business management classes later."

For the first time in weeks, Jaime's lips curved in a natural smile. She slid off the couch, walked over to Mac, and knelt down in front of him. "You already know the finer things in life, Mac." Her eyes glittered with her love. "Mister, you've got plenty of class, and the only tutoring I'm going to do is teach you to say 'Jaime, I love you, will you marry me?' Just a few simple words," she whispered, tipping her head to one side. "Think you can handle that?"

Mac groaned, reached out, and hauled her into his arms. "Jaime, I love you, will you marry me?" he repeated in a ragged whisper, burying his face against her neck as he cradled her against his chest.

Drawing back, she couldn't resist a mischievous smile. "No more throwing my background in my face?"

"Never," he vowed, a little wary of her ignoring his proposal.

"And I get my job back?" she pressed, daring to ask. "Maybe even a raise?"

Mac flexed his jaw in impatience. "Damn it, Jaime, I don't know how much more I can take," he gritted, tightening his arms around her.

She laughed and threw her arms around his neck, pressing kisses over his face.

"You know very well I'll marry you," she said happily. "In fact, I intend to keep you my prisoner. I'm not taking any chances on you changing your mind. You're stuck with me, John MacMasters, for the next hundred years."

"Play your cards right and I'll renew your contract for the next hundred after that." He wrapped his hands around the back of her head and pulled her against him. "And the next—and the next." Each word was punctuated with a hard kiss.

Jaime's lips eagerly parted, her tongue sparring with Mac's. Cool air assaulted her back as he easily negotiated her dress zipper downward and slipped the silk off her shoulders. She was just as busy unbuttoning his shirt, seeking the warmth of his skin.

"Jaime," Mac gasped, lowering his hands to cup the aching fullness of her breasts and lifting them to the molten touch of his tongue. "Pretty soon you'll have to be prepared for an overnight guest, hell, for the rest of the weekend until the license bureau opens on Monday."

She drew away from his embrace and stood up, reaching down to pull him to his feet. Smiling brightly, she slipped his shirt off his shoulders.

"Stay with me," she invited in her most provocative voice. "After all, you don't have a dog or cat to feed or plants to water or even an angry wife waiting up for you."

"Oh, I'll have the wife part soon enough." He finished sliding her dress down past her hips and to the floor. "But she'll never have to worry about me coming home late because all my evenings are going to be spent with her." He picked her up and carried her to the bedroom.

Jaime's lips curved in a warm smile as she linked her arms around his neck and tipped her head back to study the face she'd never tire of looking at. "Promise?"

"With my life."

All-new

Candlelight Newsletter

**An exceptional,
free offer awaits readers
of Dell's incomparable Candlelight Ecstasy and Supreme Romances.**

Subscribe to our all-new CANDLELIGHT NEWSLETTER
and you will receive—at absolutely no cost to you—exciting, exclusive information about today's finest romance novels and nov-
elists. You'll be part of a select group to receive sneak previews of
upcoming Candlelight Romances, well in advance of publication.

You'll also go behind the scenes to "meet" our Ecstasy
and Supreme authors, learning firsthand where they get their
ideas and how they made it to the top. News of author appear-
ances and events will be detailed, as well. And contributions from
the Candlelight editor will give you the inside scoop on how she
makes her decisions about what to publish—and how *you* can try
your hand at writing an Ecstasy or Supreme.

You'll find all this and more in Dell's CANDLELIGHT
NEWSLETTER. And best of all, *it costs you nothing*. That's right!
It's Dell's way of thanking our loyal Candlelight readers and of
adding another dimension to your reading enjoyment.

Just fill out the coupon below, return it to us, and look forward to receiving the first of many CANDLELIGHT NEWS-
LETTERS—overflowing with the kind of excitement that only
enhances our romances!

Return to: DELL PUBLISHING CO., INC.   B255A
      Candlelight Newsletter • Publicity Department
      245 East 47 Street • New York, N.Y. 10017

Name_____

Address_____

City_____

State_____Zip_____

Candlelight Ecstasy Romances™

$1.95 each

At your local bookstore or use this handy coupon for ordering:

DELL BOOKS
P.O. BOX 1000, PINE BROOK, N.J. 07058-1000

B255B

Please send me the books I have checked above. I am enclosing $_____ (please add 75c per copy to cover postage and handling). Send check or money order—no cash or C.O.D.'s. Please allow up to 8 weeks for shipment.

Name _____

Address _____

City _____ State Zip _____